The Devil's Deadly Game

A Ben Ford Mystery

ଚ ଚ ଚ ଚ

RAYMOND CAPUT

PLOT BOOKS CAMBRIDGE MASS

Cover by Mike Belcher
Interior by Myra Summers

Plot Books
The Plot's The Thing
ring.bellcaput@icloud.com

Proudly printed in the United States of America

One

BEN FORD GAZED AWAY from the Boeing aircraft bearing the American Ambassador returning from Saigon, and towards an airline hostess, neatly dressed, apparently preparing for her next flight.

A band nearby played "San Francisco," the words flowing in Ben's mind, "open your Golden Gate," as a siren sounded in the distance. The leader waved for the band to stop, but the music continued for a few bars.

A sign fluttered in the breeze. It carried the greeting, "Welcome Ambassador Pope."

The previously observed hostess was pushed closer to Ben. He was tempted almost to say, I know you, don't I?, dismissing the thought when she turned away abruptly. There was a striking beauty in her face, he noted in the fleeting moment that he observed her.

The Boeing, Flight 404 from Saigon headed towards the crowd of greeters. It taxied to a designated marked spot where its flight from Hawaii would end. Ben made his way along the crowd as the police stood protecting the area. He showed his diplomatic identification to a sergeant and took a discreet position away from and behind several dignitaries.

Along the warm air came the shout: "Welcome, Pope!"

And in retaliation sounded: "Welcome the Hawk!"

When Ben turned he could not observe the point of discord, but saw a white paper banner, flung wildly upwards, float slowly to the rear of the crowd.

The screech of the siren increased. The band unexpectedly blared forth a martial tune. The plane taxied closer to its point, its jets adding to the jumble of sounds.

The faces at the fuselage door held strained expressions. The shouts from the steward indicated a problem existed. The noise finally diminished and the music stopped abruptly.

Edging forward Ben made his way between the assembled dignitaries and several policemen.

"What's up?" Ben called to the steward, a lean man with curly hair.

"Who are you?" the steward shot back.

Ben showed him his identification. "I'm here to meet Ambassador Pope."

The man shook his head gravely. "Bad news," he said.

"What do you mean?" Ben shot back.

"I'm sorry to have to tell you," the steward spoke.

Ben muttered incoherently. "He's ill?" he asked hesitatingly.

"Worse than that–it looks like he's dead," the steward slowly replied and saw the stunned disbelief flash in Ben's face.

"Hold off. No one gets in and no one gets out," the steward recovered and spoke officially. "Get the police to clear the area. A call's been put in and these are our instructions." It was evident the steward would hold his ground.

As Ben turned, he observed that the airport police were clearing away the crowd.

The loud speaker boomed: "Special Flight 404 from

Saigon and Hawaii has momentarily been detained from unloading. We thank you for waiting."

"What are you going to do with sixty-three passengers?" a voice sounded from inside the fuselage opening.

"Question sixty-three people to find out who did him in," a man with gnarled hands spoke. He was the crew chief.

"Call some detectives," another voice spoke unkindly. The speaker did not realize his voice could be heard by others.

"There's enough for all of them," he continued. "I was up front..." His voice faded off into the fuselage.

Ben could not help thinking, what in the hell is going on? It seemed somewhat like the distortions of images in a fun house mirror; suddenly he was caught up in an occurrence which struck him as being unreal. He was here to meet the Ambassador. Who was to say that this would be changed?

His mental hostility was jarred back to reality by a sudden stirring at the terminal entrance as a group of policemen pushed their way forward.

Detective Jock Gumper, whom Ben recognized, led the way, his jacket flying in the wind, and with his tie loose about his collar so that the button showed. He was a huge man with a barrel chest and massive biceps. Gumper still retained the agility of his days as a wrestler.

Ben identified Jock Gumper from the crowded group immediately. He and Gumper worked together on a matter of importance to the State Department; and with success.

The matter of importance was the trouble that arose from the failure of one clerk to dispose of documents properly and from a snooping, unpatriotic individual who caught on to an idea for selling unburned, shredded papers to an agent of a foreign country.

Ben was relieved to see Gumper.

"This is a hell of a turn, Ben. Do you have any ideas why anyone would have the reason to commit this crime?"

"I didn't realize it was that bad," Ben replied. "I heard only comments from the crew."

Gumper continued. "The report we got was he could have been shot. You have no idea."

"None at all," Ben said. "There's the usual cranks we run into. Or anyone who took a different view of our policies. Or it may go deeper; something we don't know about." Ben recollected the rather hasty return of Ambassador Pope from Saigon. It caught Ben by surprise and shook him away from his trip up into the Sierras.

"He was flying alone, Gump. It's necessary to secure any papers he might have been carrying. Under the circumstances we're facing, I've got to make sure nothing goes wrong here."

"Okay, Ben. Let's see what we find. Maybe we can straighten out a few things." Gumper motioned Ben to follow. "The Federal offices have been advised. Where I was already at the field, Malcolm asked me to cover for him and hold things tight."

With difficulty, since Gumper moved ahead, Ben caught the detective's words. "There's a chance we'll find powder burns on somebody's hand."

Gumper entered first, followed by Ben and several others Gumper asked along. They walked to an isolated section of the plane reserved for the Ambassador. Joshua Pope remained as the steward found him.

At first appearance, it seemed Pope might be dozing, his chin forward on his chest and his right hand thrust down upon his knee, below which a book had fallen from his grasp. It was the book that interested Jock Gumper. He leaned forward and wedged downward carefully as much as his large frame would permit him. He remained in this position for a while and let out a mild sigh when he concluded his investigation.

"When we can move some of what's here, we'll see pretty well what has happened."

"Why the book?" Ben inquired.

"It is more than a book, Ben." His face showed a puffy redness from having bent over in an awkward position.

"I would say quickly that the book was a carefully contrived device, set to fire into anyone who opened it. For the time being, I'm assuming it was intended for the Ambassador."

The fired bullet had, from all indications, struck Joshua Pope in the chest causing a quick death. The Ambassador had no time to call out or seek assistance. The blood from the wound spread out along the Ambassador's white shirt.

A general murmuring started amongst the passengers, impatient to be released and on their way to complete their travels. Yet their cooperation was evident to Ben. They realized they were traveling with an important high—ranking person.

Gumper spoke briefly with the Captain of the Boeing. When they were several hours away from their arrival in San Francisco, they became aware of Ambassador Pope's death. The stewardess spoke with him a short time prior, so the time of his death was placed to be from two to three hours before arrival at the West Coast terminal.

Ben knew that each passenger would be questioned. The book could have been handed to Ambassador Pope in Vietnam prior to his departure. Or, for that matter, Hawaii. The means taken to kill Pope, if it was an assassination, seemed particularly bizarre; and despite the fact the method employed appeared successful, Ben wondered if the attempt failed, could other means of execution awaited the Ambassador.

Gumper released the crew and passengers with the instructions that they must remain at Customs to await some questioning.

For a while Ben remained at the terminal. He gathered up all the papers belonging to Ambassador Pope. He placed them in safekeeping. Gumper was of considerable assistance here. Ben called his Washington office to clear various matters with his boss, Mark Crescent. Crescent's secretary, Miss Neal, had been trying to reach Ben and advise him Mark was raging. At which Ben cursed.

Kyle Sanders in San Francisco, in the local State Department office, said he received word from Washington that Pope was onto something important enough for Pope to return from Saigon.

"How did you come in on it, Ben?" Kyle asked after his arrival on the scene.

"I was vacationing for a few days. Washington said to hop down to meet Ambassador Pope. And then this happened." Ben had not expected Pope's return so soon from Saigon.

"I recall you worked with the Ambassador," Kyle said. Sanders was in his forties; had an aquiline face, a rather thin body, but well proportioned. He had that frame on which any suit fitted well. "I think you were the only one who could get away with calling him Josh, if you wanted to."

Ben would not have put it that way but he accepted the fact his past relationship with Ambassador Pope was excellent. Because of Pope's sensitive assignment, he could at times act short-tempered. But he still was very much admired and seldom criticized by those who worked with him.

"He was the best," said Ben. "It's hard to realize what has happened."

Kyle nodded. "Now the question is why? Must be related with his returning to Washington. It's a very good possibility," Kyle said. "Do you think we will be cut in on it shortly?"

"Maybe." They crossed from the office they were in to observe Gumper from a distance as he spoke with the passengers, one by one. Ben continued talking. "He certainly showed a great knowledge of what was occurring throughout the world. The newspapers treated him well, and fairly, but never seemed to understand his full value and range of knowledge."

"What especially?"

"You can't put your finger on one thing. It was his total vision. If you want to select one point, you might consider his position on the European Communists. He worried less about them than other regions of the world.

"The thought Pope had was that Russia must eventually move towards closer cooperation with the other European countries."

Jock Gumper now joined them.

"We think we've done as much as possible for the present," he said, "although I don't have any solution." It was not on a note of embarrassment. There was something suggestive in his expression that caught Ben's attention. Having worked with Gumper before, Ben guessed Jock might have a plan in mind, some avenue of approach.

Gumper continued: "Ben, can you drop down to the lab this evening? After you've cleared up your business."

"I got to thinking, Ben. This thing looks big and I want to move as speedily as possible. But how, where, you know?" Gumper pounded his heavy fist upon the desk. "I have little to go on. But it's tough in a situation of this sort. The Federal personnel are conducting their own investigation. It's understandable they would have more information. About Ambassador Pope. Reasons for security. Still this comes under our jurisdiction. Since nothing has been definitely determined, he died–or was murdered–in San Francisco. It's as much a matter for the San Francisco police as anyone." His agitation showed in the determined look of his eyes. "I asked Sanders to speak to..." he continued, looking to Ben for the name.

"Mark Crescent."

"Crescent, right. I like him to give me more range on this case. I realize the diplomatic security and so on. I don't want to be overstepping any bounds or trampling on somebody's foot, you understand."

"I wish we could work together on this, Gump." For the first time that day, Ben began to relax; he could now look at the situation objectively. The evening was warm and comfortable. The walk from his hotel calmed him. The thought troubled him he had not been in a position to protect Pope. Ben was determined that he would find a solution.

"You know my position by now, Gump. Perhaps it is a coincidence for the two of us to be thrust together again. I've worked for the Diplomatic Corp these past two years and I'm thankful I could rely on you for assistance when I needed it."

Gumper stripped the cellophane wrapper from a cigar. He placed a lit match to the cigar. He considered the reason he asked Ben over. The brawny man squinted his eyes through the smoke.

"It's my opinion, Ben, we must start with the occupants of the plane first. The thought isn't necessarily elementary, either. One opinion was offered me this afternoon that, since the planting of the book brought attention immediately to one of the passengers being suspect, we most likely would have to go outside for the answer. The idea being no murderer would want to be caught in a tight little compartment even if there were other passengers to suspect. And this is good reasoning except that the urgency might have existed in some plan to eliminate the Ambassador. If that is so, he, she, or they must work hurriedly. Someone, we'll say, books on the trip knowing that Ambassador Pope will be a passenger. Pope's trip was no secret?" Gump asked.

"It was known he was returning to the States," Ben replied.

"It was known in both Saigon and Hawaii then," Gump said. "Until it can be confirmed, I'm only assuming he was carrying important information, even vital, if he need be murdered because of it. The party would board the plane with the express intention of preventing the delivery of the information. X is given the job to stop Pope. That's so far as we can go now, assuming we're on the right track. We don't know where the party got on or whether it was a man or woman. So, it's X."

"We can't eliminate the possibility the book was handed to him before his departure," Ben said.

"I know," Gumper agreed, "but, keep in mind, if a party wanted to do away with Pope, they didn't have to be so careful. Pack a bomb for him, blow up the plane, anything like that. You see what I mean?"

Ben nodded. "You're thinking X was on board and did not want to go down with the ship."

"Right." Gumper wiped his brow. The office was warm. The sky had darkened and the artificial light reflected on his face. "X, they, whoever wanted to work quickly, and this device was planned for just such an occasion."

"The thing that knocks your whole idea to hell is if we're dealing with a bona fide wacky person. You know that." There was no satisfaction in this remark for Ben, but the person with no cause was always the possibility.

Gumper shook his head. "I doubt it, but I agree we can't dismiss the idea. There are other distressing possibilities. To mention one, there is the possibility the book was not intended for him. We would have to consider other ideas." He swung around in his chair so that he was facing the windows, and searched through some papers that lay on a desk. He waved a sheet before him, turning back to Ben. "This is a list of the passengers and crew. Just considering the passengers, we have sixty-three people." He set the paper before him on the desk. "I've got Jacob Cardi on this. We've put together all the information we could compile on short order for each of the passengers. This is what I was spending the afternoon on. Cardi is a whiz at this. You know. We have more information coming in from other points. Cardi will assemble all the facts, considering the sensitive points especially. He's working on it now, making a record on each person. Then, we'll feed it to the computer. We are looking for the facts and background which will more closely fit a suspect, or suspects. To my mind, it's our best chance. We had no luck with powder burns," he concluded.

The application of the computer's mechanical brain to problems of this sort worked before, Ben knew. It was worth the effort.

Two

IT WENT UNNOTICED FOR MANY, the brief dispatch as it appeared in the Paris paper. The newspaper, Le Soleil, quoted Hsinhua, the Chinese press agency, which spoke about the foreigner who had come to visit Tao Sing in a little town outside Tientsin. In a somewhat garbled fashion, the visitor to the town was referred to, as best as the Paris correspondent could make out, as a Gregory Stavros. The newspaperman explored it no further. He was completely unfamiliar with the name and when his inquiry to the Communist newspaper brought no real reply but an apparent evasive answer, he pursued the matter no further. If he had gone forward with his inquiry, he might have learned more interesting facts, but not enough to reveal to him the importance of the discussions going on between Stavros and Tao Sing.

The warm sunshine bathed the hills of the small hamlet outside Tientsin that afternoon when the discussion was held which eventually would affect many lives.

"The work of the past years will bear fruit," Stavros said. "And, mind you, Sing, when one considers the work of this undertaking, the expected reward is not that great in comparison."

"Except you could be in control of drugs," Sing rebuked him mildly. Some time passed since Stavros shook off his own drug addiction, but the recollection of his earlier days still plagued him. He did not forget the revelations, that came while under the influence of the drugs. Advised to stop by his physician, it became an extremely trying and maddening experience. He maintained a positively charming, sociable appearance while his mind formed the worst and the weirdest plans.

He dabbled in many vices which proved uninteresting. The narcotics business interested him since it could be controlled at the source where it offered less competition.

"I can heartily agree with you," Stavros went on. "I enjoy the pleasant thought of success."

"There is some chance for error," Sing said testily. His demeanor was not as mild looking as Stavros' was. It was the look of the quieter days of the Orient but also reflected the businesslike attitude of the city man. Stavros was no less a businessman and a bargainer, but he concealed his hardness.

"I leave no chance for error. That's the way I plan. Why plan otherwise? One plans for success. So, I plan for success." Sing found him difficult to question in this regard and he accepted Stavros' firmness.

"Well, then, the date has been set, we agree?"

"Yes," Stavros replied.

"And the time?" Sing asked.

"At three o'clock in the Eastern section of the United States. This will allow the concurrent experiments throughout the country." Stavros smiled. It was in consideration of experiments. Experiments was a most applicable word for him. It relieved the conscience he might have.

He regarded Brier at Cape Kennedy with a certain degree of cold fondness. This would apply as well to Brozto in Detroit. The others were of little interest. Yet the expendability of them all concerned him not in the least.

Sing must remember Stavros' admonition: "The less that remains, the more secure our position later."

The application of this advice to Sing was the greatest concern of Stavros. In his craftiness, and unerring knowledge of the thoughts of others, he noticed Sing's hesitancy and suspicions. He refrained from mentioning the value of eliminating all witnesses and spoke more passionately of Sing's indispensable contributions to their joint venture.

Never did the size of the undertaking enter into the thinking of either Stavros or Sing. Sing felt he had a score to settle; the insults of his past life, the failure of recognition in his field of Chemistry and Physics. He was willing to work outside his authority to settle these marks. In Stavros, he found an ally and the opportunity he hoped for. He realized that, without Stavros, he would find no personal satisfaction. Stavros as well could not successfully conduct his affairs without the assistance of Tao Sing.

Together they sat contemplating their hoped for success. As promised, Sing, whose position enabled him to control extensive power, would look to the satisfaction of Stavros' plans.

Beyond the forces that Sing could command to obtain the needed materials and equipment for Stavros, his further value to the operation was in his expertise on matters of physical chemistry. He also arranged for the use of sea crafts and to facilitate their work, the device of an importing front.

Sing would not make a conclusion on what their success primarily depended. It was not that simple. Each part played was very important but could not stand alone. Sing would never smile or laugh at the serious business as Stavros might.

Almost as in sync with their mental attitudes, the hillside was suddenly enveloped in a blackening squall. The rain fell heavily, pouring down the slopes, forming little rivers of water; the wind flung the trees of the nearby grove about. A shutter on one of the windows loosened and smashed back and forth noisily against the side of the small building.

A number of peasants moved out of the fields where they were tilling and tending the soil. Their bare chests were wet from the heavy rain. Their faces still showed more the sweat of toil than the rain which was shielded from their faces by the tattered straw hats they wore. On the older men, the gray mustaches and goat-like beards made them appear as etchings of the unchangeable past. One rather disheveled peasant gazed steadily towards Stavros.

Stavros did not notice him particularly amongst the rest of the plodding workers. His eyes traced the distant Eastern horizon from where the ominous clouds drifted in. He recalled the churning waves and salty spray of the Yellow Sea and something of the powerful forces of nature. In time, perhaps he would be atomized into the elements of nature; such forebodings troubled him.

"You will be leaving shortly?" Sing asked.

"Yes, within the next two weeks," Stavros replied, his face ashen in the darkness. The sound of the rain darkened his spirit, it made him melancholy.

Sing observed the somber mood of Stavros, and the pause in their discussions. Their talk should be terminated.

"I shall make the arrangements then," Sing spoke as he drank some wine. "Let me know the exact date for the boat to be ready."

Stavros nodded. His attitude changed abruptly. He reflected on his impending trip on the yacht. This means of transportation worked so well in their plans and was the reason the correspondents in China did not reply to the Paris correspondent. They did not know how Stavros arrived. On inquiry to higher-ups, they learned to contain their curiosity. They used the discretion of a controlled society and shut their mouths, eyes and ears.

At somewhat the same time, Ben Ford was reading the newspapers. He did not see anything of the Paris correspondent's reports. If he had read it, he would certainly have given it little attention.

The article in the *Times* interested him, however. It spoke of a psychiatrist's warning of the possible misuse of hypnotism over television, cautioning that a person could be placed into a hypnotic trance with television as the vehicle for the hypnotist. It actually worked in experiments with the subjects being induced into hypnotic slumber with the usual instructions, the usual closing of the eyes and relaxing. Then the subjects were left with post-hypnotic suggestion which only the physical touching of the person who induced the trance could remove.

The importance of the article was its relation to what Stavros and Sing had been discussing.

The importance of the hypnotism to Stavros was a major consideration in his scheme. While in the States, he learned about it, and applied it with success. Others helped in the perfection of his work, both knowingly and unknowingly. It worked and would again, he assured himself.

The consideration of making use of a yacht for travel came about from discussions between Sing and Stavros. Sing explained to him that, if the secrecy that Stavros desired in his travels was so important, then he might consider the use of a craft Sing had available to him for research purposes. It would go beyond the yacht's intended use but Sing assured Stavros that the arrangement could be managed without questions being asked. Boarding and disembarkation would be made at sea, short distances from shore with the coordination of small motorized boats to assist at the points of arrival and departure. Stavros was so taken up with the idea when it was first proposed by Sing, and having witnessed its initial success, he decided to employ this mode of travel in his future undertakings. If not a yacht, which in this case was made possible because of Sing's unique position, then a smaller seaworthy vessel would do. The entire idea meshed with Stavros' conviction that disrupted methods of travel would counter others from tracking his whereabouts, or certainly confuse them.

Stavros followed the line that two requirements were absolutely necessary in his ventures; trust no one completely, and the other, maintain secrecy at all times. He had the means available to him. He amassed a considerable amount of money over the years, participating in the buying and selling of munitions and the equipment of war. He worked with every party in the game at the time. There were occasions he was involved in selling to both sides of a conflict.

Stavros journeyed to Tientsin after he arrived in Manila. He started with a prearranged meeting with Sing's yacht off the northern end of Luzon. His trip took him past Formosa, into the Yellow Sea and to the Gulf of Chihli. He would now return to Manila through the same waters and resume his identification there as if he never left. This was the secrecy that he strove for and that now was an integral part of his operations.

As they rode along to where Stavros would make his departure, the latter noticed the disheveled person who appeared earlier among the peasants but was who not seen at the time by Stavros.

"He stands out among your other employees. Who is he?" Stavros pointed over to where a man with long hair was standing along the road and apparently gazing expressionless in their direction.

"Chen," Tao Sing replied quietly. "A lab technician. He has great promise, I think."

"To be trusted?" Stavros asked.

"Oh, yes," Sing answered. "We checked everyone–

closely. Why do you ask?"

"He seemed to be looking this way, towards us; everyone else we passed showed no interest. Curious," Stavros spoke, "I always look for the curious, the slight defect in an otherwise perfect painting."

Sing smiled understandingly, but did not respond. Their vehicle continued along the road. They lost sight of Chen and the other people near him. Finally, they arrived where Stavros would take his leave. The usual pleasantries were exchanged, the shaking of hands, and Stavros departed.

Three

On Tuesday it was raining and dismal. Ben had his breakfast at the hotel and felt better about the approaching day.

The papers generally covered the occurrence of the previous day in a fair fashion; sometimes, it was possible to learn a bit of information on some subject that was overlooked.

It was Sanders' words that Ambassador Pope was returning with something big. Stated this way, the mind could conceive the worst which was undoubtedly the intention of the expression.

It would be interesting to see what Gumper and Cardi learned from the computer and whose names the computer would select. Ben did not take any particular note of the plane's passengers the previous day. What could he say but that they appeared to be the usual world travelers about to disembark from a long trip. No reports had come from anyone to say so-and–so behaved unusually during the trip. Sort of simple until you started to dig in and Gumper's approach was as good as any.

Cardi would examine each person by their name, nationality, age, profession, point of origination, final destination, time out of the States, etc., allowing so much value to each item, feed the amassed information into the computer and wait for its answers. Thus, from a hodgepodge of facts and information would come the organized classified result. Ben had a deep respect for the process and the automatic calibration that eliminated much drudgery and loss of time.

Slipping on his raincoat, not forgetting to stuff a pouch of tobacco and a pipe into his left pocket, he departed the hotel and walked a short distance through the rain until he caught a taxi to Kyle Sanders' office.

"Wet out, Ben," Sanders spoke, watching a few drops of water shed from Ben's coat onto the thick red carpet. "The old man wants you on the line." This was Mark Crescent's line from Washington; the conversation garbled in transmission but was received clearly on the opposite end. The three hours' difference meant it was close to noon on the East Coast.

"What does he want? Do you know?"

"He spoke to Gumper last night. Wants to talk to you about it."

The call went through in short order; however, there was a slight delay to get Crescent free to answer and on the phone.

Clarissa Neale's voice sounded cheerfully in his ear. "He will be with you shortly." She was a sweet little actress, Ben knew. He could imagine her cupping her hands over the mouthpiece and furtively saying, "Ben, wonderful to hear your voice. I can't wait to see you again. You better not forget Clarissa—ever, you understand?"

"I do, Clarissa," Ben beamed back. "Now, please get me Mark Crescent."

If ever one had troubles, Clarissa could make you forget them. It was her happy, expressive voice and her sweet, lovable eyes and face. She could endure everything, it seemed, except Crescent's habit of cursing.

"Ben," Mark spoke in a slightly agitated voice. "Spoke

to Jock Gumper last night. He is of the opinion he can do something for us. How do you feel about it?"

"I'm all for it," Ben replied.

"Well, it's not that simple," Crescent continued. "I am making some arrangements so that he can work along with you. You can expect every possible cooperation from this office. It may mean some expense. Don't worry about it. Sanders will have whatever you need for now." His words continued with great import. "That came down from the top. You know what I mean. Some embarrassment here. Understand? We need results."

"We've started on one approach."

Crescent listened attentively and patiently as Ben explained.

Crescent spoke: "Good, good. Ben, listen carefully."

"Yes."

"Ben, we don't believe we have complete information on what Ambassador Pope was on to. Sanders went through the few papers he was carrying, but they shed no light on what we're after. Everything is being sent on here including his personal belongings. I would like to have a meeting with you and Jock Gumper on Thursday, ten a.m., here in Washington. If anything breaks in the meanwhile, please advise me. Ten a.m., Thursday," Mark Crescent repeated.

Ben confirmed: "We'll be there at ten a.m. on Thursday."

"Don't forget to keep in touch if anything develops," were Mark Crescent's parting words.

He knew Gumper would be pleased. The latter had shown an intense interest in the case; he would be happy to have a shot at solving a problem. And both of them would undoubtedly be made cognizant of the facts surrounding Ambassador Pope's return. Ben felt the anxiety in containing his curiosity. He wanted to know.

"You're satisfied the way this has turned out?" Sanders

asked.

"I intend to find out who killed Ambassador Pope. And anyone who had a part in his murder."

He thought it was a startling revelation that Washington apparently did not have the full information on what Ambassador Pope learned. It was too early for conjecture. Still he guessed that what might have transpired was that Joshua Pope was returning as planned, and possibly uncovered some additional important information, sometime prior to departure from Saigon.

It was important now to arrange his schedule and system of contact with Kyle Sanders. The plans were made so that Kyle would know Ben's moves and whereabouts, and would be able to transmit to Ben any vital information and necessary money. The balance of the day was spent on this coordination, with Jock Gumper being given an opportunity to voice his approval. Gumper was in total agreement, having cleared with his office for this special assignment. Mark Crescent carried out his work well, and the San Francisco police yielded the use of a good man. They held a particular interest in the matter. Their cooperation was very good.

Gumper's eyes reflected his excitement and satisfaction. He lived for this sort of thing. Something that could challenge his imagination. He waited patiently now for Cardi's results. The Thursday meeting scheduled in Washington allowed very little time for an answer. He had tremendous faith in Cardi who could work feverishly when the occasion demanded.

The clerk at the Hayden Hotel said, "A party has been trying to reach you, Mr. Ford, several times. Sounded kind of urgent, you know."

"Did he leave a message?"

The owlish eyes of the clerk betrayed him. "Begging

your pardon, Mr. Ford. It was a woman. Didn't leave a message, you know." The clerk inferred something by this, but was uncertain. The work at the hotel was a splendid job for him. It made up for an otherwise humdrum existence. Here, his imagination could flow wildly. Basically, he liked people very much.

Ben thanked him and caught the elevator to the tenth floor where his room held a tremendous panoramic view of the city. San Francisco sparkled outside. The colored lights flickered in the dark wet night. He wanted one last fling in the old city, at least, for this trip. He would not set any murderous pace, that was not his way, but he would manage to get around and enjoy himself. An idea ran through his mind as he gazed straight out into the black canopy of night above the city that he would be employed elsewhere for a while.

He showered, dressed for an evening out, except for his jacket which he kept draped over a chair, ordered two extra dry martinis, and settled back in a Hayden chair, while the soft music of one of those radio stations which broadcast uninterrupted melodies played. A tapping sounded at his door.

There was a catch in his throat when he observed his unexpected visitor.

"Please, Mr. Ford, may I come in?" the woman asked.

"Mr. Ford, I must see you," she said. "I was on the plane. My name is Talya Laylo."

Ben took her coat and hat, and asked her to be seated. She wore white sparkling sandals covered by transparent plastic protectors. In her face there was something of the East, the Orient.

"It is difficult for me to come this way." Her speech was clear, without any accent, so that Ben wondered if this were not an accent, the cultured pronunciation and deliberate words. "Please let me explain first who I am. I am an entertainer appearing here at the hotel, the Candy Room."

Which was located above as the penthouse gathering

place; had a very friendly atmosphere, Ben knew.

"Yes, I remember now. Your picture on the display below."

"I dance, Mr. Ford. They call me 'La Scimitar.'" Ben lowered his gaze from her eyes to her shoulder line and understood the derivation of her title. "The 'La'," she continued, "is out of place but my agent insisted on this name and I could not refuse."

"The occurrences of yesterday troubled you?" he asked.

"Yes, terribly," she replied. "It was an awful thing. That poor man, that poor, kind man. So pleasant and now so dead. What chaos we seem to be coming to. These are most difficult times. We have much to endure."

"I almost agree," Ben allowed. "Things do look difficult and bad, but every time had its problems."

"Yes, I know," she said. "But now we play for keeps," she said with a feeling of frustration. "There is no return from this adventure if we go on. You see, I have spent most of my life in the East. I know what death and destruction mean."

"The Europeans have suffered terribly at times, too." Ben realized they had slipped into a discussion away from the purpose of her visit.

"I'm sorry," she said. "I did not mean to confuse you."

"You must believe me when I say you don't," he assured.

Ben ordered more martinis to be brought up since this was to her liking.

"You have a pleasant place here," she said.

"Yes, I like it." Ben removed his robe and put on his jacket.

"My room is above on the twelfth floor. It is pleasant too. They are very nice to the entertainers. You must see the room if you have the opportunity."

"I would very much like to."

"You must," she sighed.

Ben wished to pursue the motive for her visit and the fact that she was on the plane—a co—passenger with Ambassador Pope. Perhaps he assumed too much too soon. If she were on the plane, she was suspect like sixty—two other people. She might fall at number sixty-three on Jacob Cardi's list, but she could be number one. What was he thinking about? Miss Talya, La Scimitar, came bearing information, she said, but they discussed irrelevancies; or had they?

"The drinks, Talya."

"Thank you."

The bellhop withdrew uneasily and with difficulty, experiencing some hesitation in gazing away from the beautiful Talya. Folding a five-dollar bill lengthwise, Ben thrust it into the bellboy's hand and ushered him out sympathetically.

They toasted and drank slowly.

"Mr. Ford, my reason for coming," she began, setting aside her glass on the smooth marble surface of a low table, "is to complete an assignment entrusted to me." She reached for her purse and, opening it, paused. "Ambassador Pope was a kind, very dear person. And I know that in fulfilling his request, I perhaps involve myself in a most serious situation. I want you to help me so that I should be protected from greater involvement."

"Has someone threatened you?" Ben asked.

"No, it is not that at all. I mean, the police, questioning, damaging publicity, things of that sort. It could be ruinous for someone in my profession."

Ben considered her plight.

"Let's say I shall do everything possible, Talya, and I am in a position to help you."

This statement had an obvious comforting effect on her. She expressed her relief and satisfaction; then withdrew an envelope from her purse, handing it to Ben.

"Ambassador Pope asked that this be given to you. He handed it to me on the plane. He said you would be staying at the Hayden. A coincidence. He seemed very grave at the time, as if he was aware of some possible danger. To think he was right, the poor man."

It was a long envelope and bore simply the address, "To Ben Ford, Hayden Hotel, San Francisco, U.S.A.", with the U.S.A. written hesitantly, appearing as an afterthought.

"You don't feel it was a suicide?" she asked. The question indicated that she did not know the contents of the envelope which was carefully sealed.

"I doubt it." He fingered the envelope's thickness, guessing there were one or two sheets of paper inside. "You have performed a great service, Talya. We are in your debt. This may serve to clarify many points, if not all."

She stood up to leave. "Thank you, Mr. Ford, you have been very kind and considerate. I only hope I have helped."

"Ben," he suggested.

"Yes," she said and smiled. "Please keep me advised on what I should do. I have my appcarances at the show this evening but shall be available later. Room 1240, you should remember, Ben."

"I shall."

"Dear Ben," the letter read. "First, I must express my deep satisfaction in your accomplishments of the past several years with the Corp. Your position has been unique and your work gratifying. I am thinking especially of your troubleshooting in Berlin and later at the Congo, which you carried out with great skill. You are a credit to this fine organization for which we work—yes, we work—let none deny it—and to the extent sometimes I feel we care naught for our health and wellbeing. So, I start with these words of Well Done and Pursue the good work as in the past.

"However, my reason in writing is not primarily for these words so deserving to you, since, after all, I look forward to seeing you personally; it is primarily a precaution on my part since, just prior to my departure from Saigon, I was given additional valuable information, and not having had an opportunity to transmit this information to Washington, enter it here.

"There is an independent organization known as Baffle working on a master plan from in China, with operators in Hanoi and Saigon and contacts in the States. It is known as Operation Baffle. Its primary purpose is to cause extensive damage throughout the States, and possibly the United Kingdom.

"They have selected certain historical monuments, shrines and structures to be damaged. What these may be I am not fully aware, except that the Statue of Liberty, Liberty Bell, and Washington Monument have been named as possible targets.

"I am sorry to say that, at this writing, I have been unable through my contact in Saigon to obtain the names of any of the agents or their principal organizer.

"This information, Ben, must be relayed immediately to Washington and all due precaution taken, which I perhaps need not mention.

"The only importance for this letter would be my incapacitation. I am hoping for the best, but am mindful of the danger involved, and, therefore, take this precaution.

"I entrust you with this task and remain, Joshua Pope." Ben reread the letter several times, doing what most people would do when they have been handed an important piece of written matter—pick out the words, the meaning in each: Operation Baffle, Berlin, Congo caught in his mind. This was new to him. Operation Baffle. Was this what Washington was on to? A messy proposition, defacing monuments, possibly maiming or killing some innocent bystanders, all for a despicable purpose. It would anger almost everyone in the country. It was a hell of a way to marshal the strength of the country. But that it would do. This obviously was not Operation Baffle's purpose; rather it wanted to prove the penetrability of the States, that it could display its vicious capabilities.

He was on the phone to Kyle Sanders for procedure.

"Kyle, I must see you. Here at the hotel."

"You would interrupt me," Kyle laughed. "I was just going out. I'll be over. How soon?"

"As soon as you can make it."

"Gumper?"

"I want to see you first."

"Okay." Abruptly, he hung up.

Ben crossed to the door of his spacious room, listened and checked the lock on the door to make certain it was secure. Scouting around, he sought a place where he would later conceal the letter, if it were necessary. When Kyle arrived he would also be given the information. Mark Crescent would want the letter, to analyze and secure it as primary information, a document for the files.

A while later Kyle arrived and he was given the letter to read. He sat digesting its contents, then took out a cigarette, lit it and fanned out the match. The cigarette hung from his lip as he talked through the pale smoke.

"How did you get it?"

Ben explained Talya's visit, the rest.

"Seems odd, doesn't it?" Kyle put in and explained. "You know, Joshua Pope doesn't strike me as being one to know a dancer."

"She didn't say she knew him that well. Asked to deliver an envelope by an important person, she did it. She was acquainted with his position. An Ambassador. What's so unusual?" Ben said. "But I can see your concern. Shall we have her covered?"

Kyle put up his hands. "Not yet. Maybe you're right and she's not going any place. I'll cover her while you're gone."

"I was afraid of that," Ben said.

"Why?"

"You haven't seen her," Ben replied. "Come on, I'm famished. We'll get a bite upstairs and catch her act."

Which they did. They ate expensively and well. The show followed.

Talya entered for her performance in a flowing white cloud of silk and spun and turned in the most artistic manner for her sleek body. The music was soft, mellow, and the whole action and sound blended into a portrayal of superfine control. The colored lights made sparkling reflections that moved.

Kyle was impressed.

"I'm sorry," he said afterwards at the tenth floor room, "I imagined a dancer to be something different. It was an artistic dance, however." And he smiled.

"You're not kind, Kyle." The phone rang and Ben answered.

"Jock Gumper, can I come up? I have Jacob Cardi's results." Shortly, there were three for a discussion.

"Cardi was engulfed with papers and facts. It was quite a chore. Much of our information came from overseas. The cooperation was excellent–right down the line." Gumper carried only a small manila envelope containing a digest of the information they were seeking. "I never cease to be bewildered with Cardi's ability. At one time, he seemed fit to be tied, but finally he has the papers together. He assembles the information, feeds it to the computer, and presto! out come the results we have been working for."

It was over twenty-four hours since Ambassador Pope's demise, and now Gumper was to present them with computerized information as to who were the most likely suspects upon Flight 404 from Vietnam and Hawaii.

"Out of sixty-three passengers and the crew, which we did not eliminate, we have selected two people," Gumper continued.

"The first one I give you is a Mr. Bartholomew Free. He is an importer, has traveled extensively in the Orient, apparently has no criminal record, but belonged to some secret Chinese organization called Pi-Lpi. But there is a suspicion he is mixed up in narcotics. We are checking on it, although he came through Customs clean. Fifty years old, he dresses well, lives and works out of Manhattan, American citizenship, Caucasian."

They listened intently to Gumper.

"Narcotics is always bad. You may have something there if it follows up," Kyle said.

"Right," Gumper nodded his head.

"The other is a healthy-looking woman. In her twenties, neat dresser, out of Hawaii, American citizen. A mixture of Caucasian and Far East. We're not too sure. She has lived in Saigon, Hanoi, different spots in Sumatra, Java and Malaya. She may be in some racket we haven't pinpointed. I'm giving you the highlights on these two, there is more background. Actually, each of the others had one or more major points of information ruling them out."

"You drift, Jock," Ben said. "Who is she? What's her name?"

"Her name is Laylo. She's a dancer, and she's known by the stage name of..."

"La Scimitar," Ben and Kyle spoke in unison.

Four

As he did with the four others, Stavros reviewed the mechanics of the operation with Walter Buswell in Los Angeles. Unknown to Buswell was the fact that he was selected as Automaton number five by Stavros who considered the designation with a certain degree of wry humor. What some chided him could not be done, was done. True, the plan was not concluded; still, the proof was here that the first requirement was fulfilled, the reduction of the individual will to a mechanically-operating device propelled by the will and determination of Stavros.

His knowledge of drugs was not wasted in this endeavor. Walter Buswell, as well as the others, was attracted by the facts that appeared on their local television. Amongst the many others who responded, they were screened and selected. It took time and patience. It could never be said Stavros lacked patience.

Their individual selection was based on their sensitive positions, their capabilities, knowledge of Chemistry and Physics, their responsiveness, and planning. In all, five years passed since Stavros first conceived the undertaking. With Tao

Sing, some doubts remained, but never with Stavros.

What followed were the application of the drugs, completely unknown to each selected automaton. The preparations called at first for mild drugs with a gradual step up until the drugs were used in conjunction with hypnotic sleep.

In the meanwhile, the treacherous work began, the stealthily entering of the mechanical parts into the installations, the fissionable material following, and, finally, the triggering device.

As he spoke to Buswell, Stavros' eyes burned with fire and determination. They entered the very final phase and the ultimate date was determined and given to each of the five. With his conclusion with Buswell, his plan of five years would then proceed independently of himself; the key at this point would have been turned and the destructive plot would grind inexorably to its conclusion.

Buswell listened obediently from his hypnotic state.

The voice of Stavros droned softly.

"We have now thoroughly covered our work, Mr. Buswell. You understand, again, that this is merely a test, that no harm shall come to you or anyone else. It is a necessary test for the good of this nation."

These were the same words Stavros repeated so often that they were etched permanently in the subconscious world of Walter Buswell. Stavros, at times, would have him repeat the comprehension that it was a test, that no harm would ensue. Continuously Stavros would specify the important date.

"On that Thursday, you will proceed from the research laboratory at precisely eleven forty-five in the morning to your office. As we know, you may expect the minimum interference at this time. But, in the event you are interrupted–say, someone stops to speak to you–you will be allowed out of the fifteen minutes to twelve noon five minutes to speak and make your apologies. As understood, your final excuse, if necessary, would be that you must contact your home before noon on a very personal matter. You shall state it this way so no one shall accompany you. The chances are it shall not be necessary. You understand?"

Buswell nodded his head impassively; his eyes stared fixedly upon the brass doorknob several feet before him.

It was a strange doorknob with antique finish and flourishes along the outside perimeter. Buswell's mind indicated that it was strange but Stavros asked him to fasten his gaze upon the knob, and what Stavros said was naturally right and good. Buswell must close his mind to all distractions and think only of the knob with the tiny edging of scrolls and the floating little figure which appeared as a nimble cherub.

"You shall remain in your office once you have reached it. Exactly five minutes before noon, you shall proceed to lock the door of your office. Under no circumstances whatsoever shall you open it until your work has been completed. Even if someone were to try to distract you with shouts of fire or other conceivable distractions. You shall remain firm in your determination to completing your work.

"You shall then assemble the several parts upon your desk; this we know as the triggering mechanism. At precisely one minute before the hour, you shall insert the mechanism into the black container in the lower drawer of your file.

"Then your work shall have been completed."

The assurance that rang in Stavros' voice was mainly for himself. Buswell could not understand the conclusion. He could stare fixedly ahead and realize only the softness and kindness of Stavros' persuasive words.

For a few minutes Stavros tilted back in his chair studying Buswell carefully. He could relish these few minutes. Time seemed so unimportant at this juncture.

Although the date was set in those five minds he had won over, he made the one precaution to have each watch for a certain commercial at eight in the morning on a television news broadcast. No one would place any value in the innocuous report of his work–it would be but a few seconds–except those he selected to understand. The doorknob would beam prominently. And to them it would mean the plan should proceed as scheduled. In the event Stavros wished to hold up on the calamitous preparations for that date, he need merely cancel the advertisement. This, he felt, would never be necessary.

When Stavros' hand reached out and touched Buswell, Walter responded with a slight shake of his head and a blinking of his tired eyes.

"It is true, then," Buswell said, uncertain of what they had been talking about. His lips twitched as he ran his hand along his forehead. "You know, I'm sorry, I almost have forgotten what was the point of our discussion."

"We were saying," Stavros spoke, "how unusual it was that certain chemical analysis did not allow for unique solutions when considered from a physical background."

"Yes," Buswell replied. "The Physical world versus the Chemical world again." He laughed at what was an oft-repeated discussion and argument between the two.

Now nothing remained of the earlier stiffness in Buswell's expression. His pleasant smile returned as he recollected their many past pleasurable discussions. Also Buswell might be thankful for the splendid check he was given for his many consultations.

When the meeting was over, Buswell took special pride in his past accomplishments while he drove speedily homeward along the coastal drive. It seemed he was unusually invigorated after these meetings. The only strange things were the taste in his mouth and the odd thoughts he wished he could recall.

The Manhattan would satisfy his thirst; the thoughts might come later.

Stavros wrung his hands pleasurably. He considered what would be his fare for the evening. Now, all might continue without any further effort on his part. He felt happily comfortable, and he remained so for some time, that is, until the message came in from Tao Sing that the information had leaked and was being carried by someone in Saigon.

Five

THAT PREVIOUS EVENING AND that morning it was agreed amongst the three at the Hayden that Sanders would maintain surveillance of Talya Laylo in San Francisco, Gumper would solo to Manhattan to seek out Bartholomew Free and attempt to get a line on him, while Ben would fly to Washington to arrange for the meeting with Mark Crescent on Thursday. The evening was not without its further incident. Gumper and Sanders had departed and it was shortly thereafter that Talya called.

"I saw you there with the other man, Ben. I hope everything went well, that is, the letter, and it has helped you. Believe me," and her voice trembled with an almost awkward sincerity, "I would do anything to help. In any way."

"You have, thank you."

She was silent for a moment. "I have just returned from the second performance." A sigh, "Tiring sometimes, the work is over for today. It is comfortable to relax now. You must see how I completely forget my profession." And an afterthought. "I promised to show you my suite. If you care to–" and she was hesitant.

"Thank you, Talya; can I take a rain check?" he replied awkwardly.

She paused. "Very well, Ben. Again, I wish you the greatest success."

Clarissa Neale was beside herself in unexpected joy. "Ben!" she screamed. Fortunately, there was no one else present. She flung her arms around his neck and pressed close to him. "You've returned. It's so long. A naughty boy for staying away so long. How we've missed you."

"Clarissa," Ben said as he lifted her arms from about his neck. "You haven't changed a bit. Except you've become more beautiful." He paused. "Now, back to the typewriter and back to work. I thought I'd catch Mark."

"Sorry, Ben, he's out on something. Has you scheduled for tomorrow." She felt the edge of her hair. "You shocked me. Never figured to see you today. You might catch Mark at Rocco's. I hate to tell you that because I figured you might take me out to dinner. He said something about getting a bite there a little after six."

"You're a gem and don't think I won't see you again." Ben was on his way to Rocco's.

"Love and kisses," she called out to him; and the tapping sound of her typewriter followed immediately.

"Sit down, Ben. Didn't expect to see you today," Crescent said and, shaking Ben's hand, motioned for him to be seated.

They were at a table midway in the spacious room. "How did you know I would be here?"

"Miss Neale."

Mark Crescent winced at the formality of the answer. The usual pleasantries were over. Ben placed Ambassador

Pope's letter neatly between them.

"I figured you might want to examine this as soon as possible."

Crescent said: "Kyle Sanders filled me in last night on the hotline. We discussed it."

"What do you make of it?"

"Let me tell you something, Ben. Of course, this would come out in our meeting tomorrow, before the assembled board, by the way."

Ben reflected his amazement. "The board, I didn't realize."

"The contents of Ambassador Pope's letter," Mark continued in a carefully lowered tone, "were nothing especially new to us. It was a repeat of what he had already informed us on. He coded to us about a week ago. Then it was decided to bring him in." He stubbed out a cigarette in the tray and meditated. "It was unfortunate."

"I don't get it, Mark, destroying monuments. Even during the World Wars care was taken where possible to avoid damage to historical buildings and the like. It's sort of ironic. But to call back Ambassador Pope."

"It's bigger than that."

They discussed the developments that followed the arrival of the plane on Monday, Gumper, Talya Laylo, and Bartholomew Free, and the investigation conducted thus far.

"Mr. Crescent, how do you do?" It was a heavy, deep voice that surged in from behind Ben. It belonged to an oversized, bearish-looking man with red cheeks and nervously flickering eyes.

"Myles Bancroft," Crescent spoke, and raised himself to take the extended hand. "Here, meet one of my associates, Ben Ford."

"Charmed," Bancroft breathed and settled in the offered chair.

"Myles has done some work for us here in Washington.

Research, we might say."

"Yes, research," he confirmed with a nervous chuckle.

"His business, of which he is the head, is in the investigation of psychological matters. Rather interesting. Myles has done some work for us on the effects of stress and fatigue on psychological behavior. It was done under sponsorship of the War Department." He turned to Myles. "You are conducting some work now, I understand."

"Yes, we are."

"How is it proceeding?"

"Very well, thank you, very well, ha ha, ahem." He would sit back when he spoke, his hands clasped before his stomach, the thumbs in a circling motion about each other. His paunchiness strained against the buttons of his dark jacket.

"What is it exactly?" Crescent asked.

"Ahem, television, Mr. Crescent. Television and its effect on the masses. It has a profound effect, yes. We have had people in different cities polling, making inquiries. It is organized beforehand, of course, ha, yes."

Mark asked: "What are you going to do when you have it assembled? Publish the information?"

Bancroft's eyelids were fixed closed and the corners of his mouth twitched for the words. "Ahem, no, no. We shall use it for consultation, advertisers, television companies. That sort of thing. Yes." He turned and grasped Ben's forearm. "Do you like Washington, Mr. Ford?"

Ben said: "I've been here before. I'm not a stranger. Yes, I find it invigorating." He leaned forward, lifting his arm slightly.

"Invigorating," Bancroft was caught up, slapping his hands in glee. "Yes, ha, ha, you may be right there. Mentally invigorating. The weather, however, can be atrocious."

Standing up, Bancroft bowed and took leave. "It has been a pleasure to see you again, Mr. Crescent, and to meet you, Mr. Ford." He ambled away towards the front entrance.

However, that was not the last Ben saw of him. Afterwards, at the Clayton Hotel, in the great lobby, amid the bustle of activity, and the split-leaf philodendrons, Bancroft stood perusing a newspaper. His lips moved, mouthing the words of apparently some article. Ben saw Bancroft but just beyond he saw someone else. He could have sworn he knew her, and to get closer he used the opportunity to approach Bancroft and speak to him. She turned her face from Ben in an obvious ladylike manner. Bancroft's grasp released the corner of the paper when Ben spoke to him and the portly man fumbled to bring the pages together again.

"My word, Mr. Ford, my pleasure again, I assure you. You have lost your friend, Mr. Crescent, I see."

"I didn't mean to surprise you like that."

"Ha, ha. No, you didn't. It was merely my intentness on what I was reading."

The bellhops sped around the lobby in their perpetual efficiency. The woman sat down and fingered a magazine. She appeared to be waiting for someone.

"I found your business interesting," Ben said, which statement was a white lie, since he vaguely recollected anything on the subject.

"Thank you, ahem, yes. I would be happy to talk to you at greater length if you wish." He smiled. "Only the phenomena, however, not trade secrets."

Ben laughed. "You know, I'm astounded by the faces I seem to recognize here."

"That is one of many Washington phenomena. May I help you?"

Ben looked at him expecting this was intended facetiously. To his surprise, Bancroft was serious and, for a change, unsmiling. He decided to accept his offer.

"Well, for instance, the beautiful woman sitting there." Ben turned towards where she was sitting.

"Aha, yes." Bancroft placed his arms behind his back

with the paper falling from his grasp so that it touched the floor. He may have expected his masculine chest to be thrust forward, but his position only tended to accentuate his corpulence against the buttons of his jacket. "That woman with the blond tresses and remarkably excellently well chiseled features, Mr. Ford, ahem, is Miss Regina Terchenka. Almost royalty, you may say. Hungarian. Here to appeal in behalf of the Crown of St. Stephen. Strange, you know, but it is held in secrecy somewhere by this country. She has been asked by her country, she remains a loyal Hungarian to the present cause even though divested of her royal rights, she has been asked to plead or prevail, if you wish, upon this country for the return of the crown. Very touchy matter considering that this country has not been on especially the best of terms with Hungary." He turned with deliberate importance to Ben. "Would you care to meet her?"

This was Ben's profound desire. In his profession, there was always the awareness not to travel too far and too fast, but her beauty intrigued him. And at the same time, he was a friendly sort of person, and much was to be learned by the continuous personal acquaintanceships of the citizens of the One World. Here, he would put his philosophy to use, the establishment of closer relationships with all countries and their representatives. He accepted Bancroft's invitation without questioning further.

"Miss Terchenka," Bancroft said, "I would very much like you to meet Mr. Ben Ford, a member of the Diplomatic Corp."

In truly the great style and culture befitting royalty, she extended her hand which Ben accepted graciously. He found her grasp warm and promising and realized, now that he was close to her, her beauty was much greater than he imagined. Her eyes, he thought, told stories of a bygone splendor and her face reflected the glory of the past.

"May I say," Bancroft continued, "that she prefers to be

called Regina."

They spoke briefly of her arrival in this country, and her work, or cause, it most likely could be called. Her voice was educated, soft and soothing. She spoke with a noticeable accent but with no hesitancy.

"Were you waiting for someone?" Ben asked. "I did not mean to interrupt you."

"I must explain," she said with some embarrassment, "that I was idling my time here before going to see one of your American movies. I find them tremendously enjoyable. But I have a secret," she laughed and the tips of her fingers touched Ben's arm, "I do not like to go too early and wait for the picture to end and the new picture to start."

"But you are like most of us. It is not fair to know the ending before the beginning."

"How true, Mr. Ford."

"May I excuse myself," Bancroft spoke. "I have an important call coming into my room." For the second time that evening, he took his leave from Ben.

Ben faced Regina Terchenka's beauty alone.

"Mr. Bancroft mentioned you were here to appeal in behalf of the Crown of St. Stephen."

"Yes," she said, "it is a situation that has existed since the last days of the war."

"Am I correct in my recollection that the crown was given over by officers and soldiers of Hungary to the U.S. Seventh Army?"

"St. Augsburg in 1945. It was a time of great distress," she replied. "The Hungarian law prevented its removal from the chest in which it was contained." Her eyes flashed with the intensity of her thoughts on this matter. "I do not think it was right for it to have been removed. For many years, it has been revered in Hungary and used in the coronation of countless kings."

"I know it must be valuable as a work of art and

treasure. Yet, I cannot understand the great concern."

She smiled and continued: "For several reasons. One, that no ceremony was understood to be constitutionally correct without the crown. And next, with the crown in our safe possession, Hungary shall then be considered safe. It is an old belief. It may seem childish to many, but these customs and beliefs do not change rapidly."

Ben assured her politely; "I certainly would not want to be one to break down customs."

"It was taken to Wiesbaden and finally elsewhere by the Western powers." With a certain reverence she said: "It is indeed beautiful. I have seen it. Of course, the history to it is much greater than I can tell now."

This was the opportunity for Ben to say, "Then I must learn more from you."

There was a warmth in her manners that soothed Ben's feelings and yet as they continued, there were times when she seemed to be overcome by some all possessing and disturbing thought that recurred in her mind. "When you think of it," Ben reflected, "this is not unusual and cannot be masked by the affected person though they may try."

"I was saying to Mr. Bancroft that you seemed familiar," Ben remarked.

"Yes," she hesitated. "But your face is new to me." Her eyes searched his countenance approvingly.

Their conversation carried them through various current affairs of which she held a great knowledge, and they talked for a while to the point that Ben felt he had taken advantage of her kindness. Still, he was overcome by his attraction to her and knew he must pursue his course further. He did not want to say it was a pleasure to have made her acquaintance, and to wish her great success on her visit to Washington, and to hope he might have the pleasure of meeting her again. It went beyond that. Her beauty and refinement had captivated him and he felt pleasantly trapped.

"Miss Terchenka," he said, "this is not an evening for movies." And he made his entreaty. "I feel so alone. Permit me to ask you to join me this evening for a drive around the town and a stop at a pleasant place where we may talk and relax."

She laughed. "You are funny, Mr. Ford. You need not be so formal. I detested the thought of going to see a picture alone." Her face revealed her satisfaction. "Might I be honest? I hoped you would ask me. Was that wrong?"

It was not wrong then or later for Ben, and it continued not being wrong for a full week until she departed for Europe and her return to her native land.

Ben knew it was not wrong the following morning when he walked a sprightly step to Mark Crescent's office and Clarissa glanced at him as if he were behaving oddly. Now, to tell the truth to himself, he knew he had been struck hard the evening before, for this morning he could not escape the thought of Regina's eyes, her joyful beautiful face, her closeness and touch when they drove around the sights of the city.

Gumper journeyed down from New York, and was present with Ben and Mark Crescent that morning. They sat before a long walnut conference table, so highly polished that the image of the person sitting opposite reflected on its surface.

At the end of the table sat Dr. Martin Flair, to whom they were all answerable, a white-haired, immaculately dressed man with a penchant for fine attire, and with a trim athletic figure.

It was said of Dr. Flair, and Ben knew it was true, that he led a very exciting, useful life. Flair married early in his years a charming, beautiful girl whom he met while both were attending the University of Michigan. An athlete in many sports and winner of many trophies which interested him little—in those days, they seemed to play more for the sheer enjoyment-he had majored in Economics and obtained his degree. Later in life, he sought and secured a degree in Law. In the course of his journeys before and after the war, he traveled far and wide the different corners of the world while working in the State Department. His knowledge of the East was second to none, and his acquaintance with the consultations at Yalta and elsewhere had given him a basis for the quick rise he saw through the ranks.

But the awful tragedy for Flair was loss of his youthful wife shortly after the end of the war. Having survived the action in Europe where he had been a colonel in an Infantry Division, he returned to what was expected to be a short assignment in England and the terribly sought reunion with Chris. They had no children, and really lived deeply for each other-as most often seemed the case.

He would find himself with the feeling of hopelessness during the years that followed. Chris, whom he had not seen for over a year, but whose letters he had warmly received and cherished, was lost in a plane crash off the coast of the British Isles. When he learned of it, his sorrow was so great that he asked for a leave, which was granted, to search the area of the crash in a boat he obtained for the purpose. With the passage of the days and the end of his unsuccessful search, he returned to London to resume his assignment and, shortly thereafter, was assigned to work with the State Department.

Now he spoke with the considerable determination that came with the experience of years. His authority was observed and respected because of the keenness of his thoughts and the clearness of his preparation and expression. To him, there was no good purpose in anything without the fullest preparation. If he were to address an assemblage of men on a matter of importance–and, in this case, the matter had the highest priority–he would not insult their intelligence with anything but the most conclusive facts and reasoning at his command.

As he sat he waited for the conversations to die down

and the attention of each of the group to fasten upon him.

The shade at the window rustled softly behind him in the slight breeze that followed from the direction of the Potomac. The gold and orange drapes, with the scenes from Greek mythology, hung equally on each side of him so that he appeared as someone speaking at a royal function.

His eyebrows arched and he gazed steadfastly at the papers before him.

"Next on the agenda, gentlemen," he spoke to the eight men besides Ben, Gumper and Crescent who sat along the table, "is the investigation being conducted by Mark Crescent. We are aware of the details regarding Ambassador Joshua Pope's death. There are several avenues that may be followed. We have covered some details in previous sessions as to how his death will affect our planning. Needless to say, we will conduct a maximum program to bring about a solution to the crime.

"Prior to Ambassador Pope's departure from Saigon, and by the way, this also was a reason why he was returning, we were advised by him of this plan by unknown saboteurs to deface and destroy certain monuments. This, aside from the sensationalism, was intended to prove that, despite our precautions and warning systems, we were still vulnerable to infiltration and destruction. If it were possible to destroy these monuments," he explained, "then the reasoning goes that it is equally possible to bring in, assemble and detonate atomic, hydrogen, fission, nuclear bombs, what have you.

"On his departure, Ambassador Pope was given additional information, we know, by one of our agents who, unfortunately, shortly thereafter was found murdered and his body left outside Saigon. We do not know for certain whether the agent was murdered for his part in this matter. We can only suspect that this was the case.

"The investigation that was conducted in San Francisco to date has revealed very little. And I might say that the plane trip from Saigon to San Francisco brought us nothing. We have no knowledge how the fake book came into Ambassador Pope's possession. There is a suspicion as to one or more of the passengers."

Dr. Flair momentarily paused, deliberately drying his lips with his handkerchief and watching the expressions of those whom he was addressing.

It was his intention to inform and instruct as quickly and as smoothly as possible. The questions could come later and they would be based on his foundation of facts and information.

"However, we have had what appears to be some very hopeful information from Mr. Gumper of the San Francisco Force of Investigators." Flair looked towards Gumper, and some eyes of the others turned towards the detective. Flair continued: "I shall term it a brilliant use of the computer. But, as with practically everything we have invented in this world, the use of these inventions, the successful use, depends upon the people who are called upon to operate the equipment. Mr. Gumper has been loaned to us for this investigation and this task, and by the use of the computer has reduced the investigation to two people–at least for the present–among the passengers upon the plane.

"It is not intended that these results are conclusive, mind you, but that it is an avenue of approach. Time will tell whether the computer has helped us. In the meanwhile, we have these leads to follow.

"The name of a Mr. Bartholomew Free who resides in New York City, has been given to us by Mr. Gumper. And the other name, we understand, is Miss Talya Laylo of Hawaii, who, you will recall, delivered Ambassador Pope's letter to Ben Ford.

"First, Mr. Gumper, what have you determined in your investigation of Mr. Free in New York?" Dr. Flair leaned back in his chair awaiting an answer.

Gumper looked grimly about him at the several expressions he noted. He gained confidence nevertheless from the cordial reception he received. He came prepared with the papers he carried along with him to the meeting. In a somewhat slower and deeper voice than Dr. Flair, he proceeded to outline the facts concerning Bartholomew Free.

"Bartholomew Free resides at *955* Preston Plaza in the Manhattan section of New York City. It's a rather small building in very good condition–a small stone building. He lives on the second floor. I made two calls at the address in an attempt to talk to him, but on both occasions he was out of town. I might also say that the door to his apartment was locked and that I tried it on each occasion. He lives alone and his habits are not particularly known by the few I talked carefully with, and in particular, the building maintenance man whom I was able to contact and speak with.

"He did say that Free travels rather extensively and he thought he was in some sort of toy business he was not sure–because of what looked like samples he was carrying and what he noted in Free's car on several occasions. He also maintains offices in the Gray Building.

"However, on the last occasion I went to visit him, he was just leaving in a Mercedes–the maintenance man pointed him out. I recalled him slightly from the picture we had taken of him in San Francisco and when I was interrogating the passengers for information. Well, he drives pretty fast, but I kept up with him and with a bit of help from the local police, whom I checked in with when I arrived in New York, we were able to track him into a little town called Barrymore in the Catskills. He stopped up there in a small isolated farmhouse at the end of a road called Benton Road.

"To tell you the truth, time was getting a little tight. I was not too sure in my mind what my approach should be. In any case, I left Free there so that I could make my preparations to get down to Washington this morning. I am certain he was unaware he was being followed.

"As a rundown on how he strikes me. He's a small fellow, with a thin build, and a fairly clean dresser. Apparently, he has no extreme habits that would become evident to the people where he lived. So this leads me to the suspicion he would rather remain to himself. Whether this is on purpose or he is the introverted type I do not know. That's thirty. I am not too sure I can help you much more at the present time. However, with your permission I would like to follow up on where I left off and bring in some conclusion on whether we should continue on this path or not."

Gumper paused for breath, but no one interrupted for it was apparent to the assemblage Gumper had additional words to say.

"Let me suggest, gentlemen, that the progress in this matter could be a little slow, and I realize, against our wishes. However, I feel, myself, if we stick to it, we'll crack some leads very shortly."

When he completed, Dr. Flair allowed a few seconds for the information as presented by Gumper to be absorbed. Flair ran his fingers through the papers again, marshaled a few thoughts, and picked up the discussion.

"Your point is well taken, Mr. Gumper. I, too, agree that the progress could be slow." His mood altered just slightly to impress everyone with the importance of his words. "But keep in mind that time is extremely important here—the possible shortness or lack of it—and we are perhaps being called on to bend more than a normal human effort to get an answer. We are aware of the urgency that Ambassador Pope attached to this matter. We can go only on the supposition that the element of time was involved. If something were to happen, that a definite date and hour would have been established. Therefore, time is most important.

"Thank you, Mr. Gumper. And may I say we all appreciate your cooperation in this matter. You have helped us considerably. We also shall not forget your work with Ben Ford in the past in San Francisco.

"I might take the opportunity to thank you both again for the extra effort and the great amount of time you exerted in that case.

"Gentlemen," Flair turned to the others, "I am speaking about Agent Kozlow who, you will remember, found that certain unburned papers, although shredded, could prove of value to a foreign service if only one has the patience to paste the papers together through many tedious hours. Agent Kozlow had the patience, and we must be mindful of the patience of others with whom we deal."

Flair sorted several sheets of paper before him and glanced slowly around at the assembled party before him. "And now, gentlemen, the matter of Talya Laylo. As you recall, she states she was entrusted with the mission of delivering Ambassador Pope's letter to Ben Ford. Some information has been compiled on her. Additional background continues to come in, but changes nothing about that which we already know. For the time being we have not approached her further. Nevertheless, she is being kept under surveillance by our San Francisco office."

He stood up and, putting his hands flat on the table, bent forward so that his words might be heard distinctly.

"What have we here then? Ambassador Pope departs Saigon for San Francisco," and he recited the facts in sequence again to lead to his conclusion. "The one thing we must find, however," he continued, "and I submit that it exists, is the actual information Ambassador Pope wished to convey to us. Certainly, he has written much in his letter that Miss Laylo delivered into our hands. But it repeats what we all know. It is our conclusion that he did have additional information, was taking the precaution to protect the vital facts on their way to us, and very possibly, entered it in another report or letter which exists unless this latter report has been intercepted and perhaps destroyed."

He rose to his full stature.

"Gentlemen, isn't it obvious that Ambassador Pope was intending to say something in his letter to Mr. Ford? And that the point he was making was that the contents of this letter and the proposed plot of the saboteurs was false, or at least incomplete in its information? I read from his letter." With this, he picked up the sheets of paper which Ben recognized as those delivered to him by Talya, and he began reading. "'Dear Ben,' here addressing Mr. Ford who he had been advised was directed to meet him at San Francisco on short notice. 'First, I must express my deep satisfaction in your accomplishments of the past several years with the Corp. Your position has been unique and your work gratifying. I am thinking especially of your troubleshooting in Berlin and later at the Congo, which you consummated with great skill.' I stop here, gentlemen." Dr. Flair stacked the papers neatly on top the others before him. "The classic double error. The first error could be unintended, we know. The second error following immediately upon the other, per our instructions and schooling, indicates that he intended the information to be false or incomplete. We all know, gentlemen, that Ben Ford has never served in Berlin or the Congo!"

Ben was determined to take advantage of the days remaining before Regina would return to her country and, deep in his feelings, he was concerned that when she did leave to continue her work in quest of the crown, it might spell the end of their brief relationship. He had seen it happen before; a deep attachment that forms between two people and appears destined for enduring friendship or more, and then, abruptly, is discontinued, for whatever reason, with expectation that it could later be resumed, but that never comes to pass.

It had not been an expected acquaintanceship. It started

with a chance meeting and introduction from Mr. Myles Bancroft. When Ben mentioned to Regina the chance meeting that occurred through Myles Bancroft introducing them, Regina protested.

"Ben," she said, "our meeting was destined to happen without his presence. I saw you earlier and you saw me in that moment you gazed over towards me—in the lobby. I could not be unladylike enough to speak to you. In a hotel lobby—never. But I always hoped you would introduce yourself. Myles Bancroft just happened to come along at that time." Regina paused as if collecting her thoughts to explain. "And Ben, I don't think you should trust that Mr. Bancroft. He's the type I think is definitely not so trustworthy. He may feel he is acquainted with me, but I do not consider him a friend. He's sort of," Regina hesitated as if she were searching for something to describe Myles Bancroft, "he seems to be someone who comes out of the dark when you least expect it, a specter, if you like."

"He hasn't bothered you?" Ben inquired, showing concern.

"No, nothing of the sort," she replied. "You know, it is more a question you feel you can trust someone. That is what I'm saying to *you*. His actions are polite and his appearance cannot be criticized. It's just what you feel lies behind the veneer."

Ben received her words of caution without comment but he wondered what caused Regina to be so unrestrained in her comments on Myles Bancroft. Bancroft seemed affable and pleasant enough when they met, but he realized Regina must have some knowledge of Bancroft that Ben was not aware of. He recalled the evening when they were strolling along the path, they stopped momentarily, her cold hand, Regina's slight trembling, and then her desire to be away from the darkness. She described Myles as a specter coming out of the darkness.

Ben wondered if this was something he did not

understand about Regina, even in their short relationship. Did she have a fear of the darkness, perhaps? Nothing of tremendous concern there. And did she just dislike a person, an attitude unlike what was expected of her? Again, nothing of great concern. He decided to put these matters out of his mind, but he accepted Regina's caution to be careful with Myles Bancroft. Before they parted that evening, they exchanged addresses with each other and how they were to be reached.

He made excuses to remain in Washington while Gumper journeyed to New York to continue his investigation. Always he felt he would return to his work, but for these few days it seemed right that he might remain with Regina.

Finally, the day came when Regina was to leave and he saw her to the airport. He promised he would see her again.

Six

FOR A WHILE, IT WAS obvious to Gumper, Ben had not been up to his best mental concentration, but a noticeable change occurred after Regina departed, with Ben taking a closer interest in the investigation. Nothing especially revealing came out of Gumper's second trip to New York to scout Bartholomew Free. Bartholomew imported toys and maintained a regular schedule of hopping in his Mercedes and chasing around to his customers. It was Gumper's admission that the little guy was difficult to follow, what with the latter's constant calls through the city and not being a tall person with his head above the crowds. Free was also a frequent telephone caller but Gumper only assumed Bartholomew was checking in with his office.

The matter that brought Ben and Gumper swiftly back together again was a call that came in from Kyle Sanders in San Francisco. Talya Laylo had run out of her engagement at the Candy Room of the Hayden Hotel the previous damp and drizzly evening, garbed in her raincoat, and vanished in the fog and darkness along the harbor, with the eerie horns blowing in the background.

"We had her covered," Kyle told Mark Crescent, "and believe me she gave us the slip–but good. It looked promising when our man tailed her to the waterfront. We figured we were coming up with some break. This was out of her pattern. She wasn't carrying anything, must have slipped her personal stuff out of the hotel on the QT. She knew she was being watched is my theory or was taking some good precautions. She really tricked us because we figured her set in place for the length of her engagement."

Crescent was fuming but he played it cool with Sanders. It was just the thought of being outwitted and making explanations to Dr. Flair.

"What about her agent?" he asked.

"Booked out of Hawaii with a local man there," Sanders replied. "We're trying, but don't expect much."

"Well, she didn't just melt away in the fog, Kyle." Crescent indicated that he was perturbed.

"No, and she didn't jump in the drink, Mark. It was planned. Our man, Dalio, said he heard a motorboat take off from the pier about a minute before he could reach the spot."

"So she booked passage for a trip, is that it?"

"Not that easy, Mark. We hopped on right away when Dalio gave us the call. Got in touch with the Coast Guard. They checked and said she was not on any ship at the docks. There wasn't much moving. They figured the motorboat and everything disappeared. But we both know damn well what could have happened."

"Then we're battling big fellows on this one," Mark said.

"If you figure, as I do, that she's on a private yacht some place on the blue waters of the Pacific."

When Mark Crescent hung up he swore, "Damn, hell, damn," out loud and Clarissa Neale clapped her hands over her ears for what she knew would follow. However, she could and would excuse her boss again, and only wished she was in the position to offer some help in these untoward situations. This was the measure of her devotion, to be concerned beyond her regular daily work.

The fact was, she knew something of what was going on, deeper than the correspondence she handled. There was the meeting the other day with Dr. Flair and Ben and the rest. Trouble was brewing. And the thing that bothered her most and gave her some sleeplessness was what she heard Mark Crescent say in an unguarded moment.

"We've got to find out what those guys are up to before some night they blow us all out of bed. Those fiendish..."

And she heard no more as she fled behind a file in the corner.

"What do you figure now?" Gumper asked Ben as they sat dining at Rocco's.

Ben laid out the white linen napkin as a battlefield and held a pencil in his hand. Thus arrayed, it helped him to think better and marshal his thoughts.

"Without rehashing what has already happened, I think the most important theory we can follow is that of Dr. Flair. We make the assumption that the letter he wrote to me was intended to be a dupe for some adversary. And we make the further assumption that, this being true, he wrote another message, the correct one, for us to receive. Let us examine these points then. I'll ask you a few questions, Gump."

Gumper nodded his head receptively.

"What do you think about Talya Laylo's story, especially considering what has happened since?"

"She may have been telling the truth, but I doubt it. I suspect she was a plant on the plane and, going on the theory you've set out about the letters, she was typically the person

Ambassador Pope feared, and hoped would get the erroneous message."

"Then, we are in agreement, Gump, except for several further considerations. She may have been working with someone else on this assignment. And she, or they, may possibly have realized this message to be the false one and intercepted the valid one. Where does that leave us?"

"Up the creek, Ben. Right up the creek."

Ben doodled some straight line figures upon the napkin.

"A message from Ambassador Pope would say something is going to happen, what else? Or, to prepare for something that was expected to happen. If the message is found, we then can take action. If it is not found, then we're dead until it does happen, which might be too late, or not being too late, we possibly can minimize the damage. What the hell has Operation Baffle got up its sleeve?" Ben asked.

"Dr. Flair mentioned one possibility, disastrous explosions within the confines of the States," Gumper replied.

"And who would you retaliate against if it happened?"

Gumper swore. "I thought of that."

"It gives some people who know this problem some worries," Ben added.

They left Rocco's and were walking along their way to the Clayton.

"Gumper," Ben spoke, "we have covered the passengers and zeroed in on Talya Laylo and Bartholomew Free. We've been remiss. The boys in San Francisco have been checking all the passengers, we know. But consider; how do we know all the passengers made it to their destination. Isn't it possible, and it may be a wild try, that if Ambassador Pope had entrusted the correct message to someone else, that passenger may have been intercepted by Operation Baffle? Otherwise, why would Talya have delivered the letter unless they had opened it, read it, were not worried about its contents, resealed it, and had her deliver it to me. In other words, there could possibly be some other person involved they're working over right now while we stand here talking."

With this thought, Gumper was prepared to take action. To plan meant to take time, and it took time to check out sixty—one remaining passengers. They formulated their plan further to check the passengers, and also to secure a check of the letter from Ambassador Pope to verify the handwriting and authenticity. They would clear matters with Crescent, and Sanders would be contacted; the search would be handled carefully so as not to conflict with other investigating agencies, but Ben had been successful on other similar occasions. His position with the Diplomatic Corp permitted him greater range than some others might enjoy.

The fat man in the blue suit scowled and shook his finger in the face of the handcuffed man. The latter was bound to a wooden chair by steel cuffs so that his arms were extended before him and he was bent over in a most painful position. The face of this man reflected the pain he was enduring. Little of the resolve within the man showed.

"He's a real son of a bitch," a thin, dark-complexioned man spoke from the shadows. He was wearing a white shirt above which was strapped a shoulder holster with the black butt of a .38 exposed. "He's not much good now. He doesn't react too much. I think, Stavros, that the drugs were too much.

The blue–suited man referred to as Stavros turned sharply to the man who had just spoken. "I am not too sure you know anything of the art of persuasion. You're crude." And he looked back to the shackled man. "The drugs always work. It's my business. I know."

"I was just giving you my opinion," the thin man said from the darkness of the room as a light played unmercifully down upon the shackled man whose strength was ebbing under the harsh treatment of the past days.

"No stone can be left unturned," Stavros continued. "I have to know if this man has learned anything and relayed it to others. Talya has already disappeared and they'll intensify their efforts now. In twenty-four hours, we're gone." He spoke derisively.

The sitting man groaned and whispered through parched lips almost inaudibly, "Something to drink."

Without noticing him, Stavros continued, "If this fool here," and he looked down at his prisoner, "does not satisfy our concern, we'll have to take him along. There is not much choice, anyway. We couldn't take the chance of leaving him in this country. He'll disappear with all of us."

The thin man, who was listening in the background, went to the refrigerator which stood in the corner and opened it. His harsh, unsympathetic profile was outlined in the momentary light as he withdrew a salami and two cans of beer and casually flung them on a table nearby. He then displayed a loaf of bread and offered Stavros to join in a repast.

"I'm afraid that is not exactly my fare, Manfred," Stavros replied. "But go on, you eat."

Manfred asked: "What happens after we leave, Stavros?"

"We'll proceed as planned. Ben Ford and the others have learned nothing," he exclaimed. "We'll be far away, if all goes well, in Albania. The fools will have performed their tasks, the destruction of five crucial installations. It is fantastic in its simplicity. I wish I could see their faces in Washington as they seek to blame someone. They'll say, 'We have the bombs and the delivery but where do we drop them?' Then Operation Baffle will have been a success."

Stavros' eyes were glassy, his face held a wild, rigid expression. No one cognizant of the background of the terroristic plan and Stavros' work in its execution, as Manfred was aware, would question his cunning and evil genius.

"And then, Stavros, our reward?" Manfred spoke for

fear that he may at that point be forgotten.

They disregarded Giorgio for the moment, but the semiconscious man could do little but listen and try to remember something of this moment, the farmhouse hidden away in the trees, and the fatal toys of Bartholomew Free.

Stavros replied: "Never fear, Manfred, your stomach shall be filled–not with that rubbish–with exquisite foods."

A new figure silently crept into the room. "I trust you will not forget me, Stavros?"

Overcoming his initial surprise, Stavros replied, "Bartholomew, of course, you will not be forgotten. Your ingenious toys have become the hardware of this planned nightmare for our friends." But, in truth, if all went as planned, few witnesses would be left alive.

The horns from the few boats moving in the harbor sounded their warnings through the impenetrable fog of that evening when Talya Laylo departed the Hayden. The message had come from Stavros that the situation for her had become precarious, especially where it was evident that Ben Ford was investigating her background. She recalled Ben had called her Talya during that last conversation on the phone. It did not matter; she knew she had been overcome by Ben Ford's kindness, and by telling Stavros, she hoped he would have her removed so that Ben might be protected from further involvement. This was a difficult thing for her to do because she felt she would never see Ben again.

It was a fact that she had failed to bring Ben to her room. This was not Stavros' scheme, since he merely directed Ambassador Pope's letter to be delivered to Ben Ford. But, once having made his acquaintance, she couldn't forget him. At least, to have seen him would have been something for her to remember.

While she waited in her room for the time to approach

for her leaving, Talya recalled the flight on the plane from Hawaii. When she boarded, she recognized Bartholomew Free standing at the forward portion of the Boeing, speaking casually with one of the plane's officers. Talya detested the sight of the small despicable man whom she had met through Stavros. After Stavros he was the most important person in the execution of Operation Baffle; he was an expert with mechanical devices and a brain in physical chemistry. His importing toys was just a cover—up for his other activities, especially the narcotics trade and, more directly in this case, the equipment, mechanisms, activators for Operation Baffle.

She had no choice but to be associated with him. Stavros would bring up the name of her brother imprisoned in Indonesia whenever she displayed some obstinacy, so that, lately, she feigned a desire for the cause while awaiting the day she might have the opportunity to express her hidden anger. Her younger brother meant the world to her, to the extent she could endure any conceivable pain and anguish.

Her instructions were to avoid looking at Bartholomew Free and having any conversation with him. Her task was to assist only when assistance was requested. What exactly Free's moves would be she was unaware, except to expect the worse and react as the others.

After his discussion up front, Bartholomew Free, with his visage beaming congeniality, strolled casually back to his seat, several books tucked under his arms.

Talya stared straight ahead, adjusting a few items she had brought along, but aware of the approaching little man. When he stumbled, he emitted a staged chuckle and recovered his balance. It was in this move Talya could observe from the peripheral vision of her eye he was satisfied with his accomplishment, and the bundle under his arm was noticeably smaller.

The Ambassador was the last to board, again displaying his appreciation to the well—wishers outside. Making his way to his seat, he spoke briefly and kindly to the passengers. Finally the plane sped upward into the blue sky over Hawaii and shortly, only the blue waters of the Pacific could be seen.

Nearing San Francisco, great consternation broke out at the part of the plane around Ambassador Pope's seat. Talya knew it was extremely serious when the Captain came out to check.

The announcement resounded from the loudspeaker: "Ambassador Joshua Pope, whom you know has been traveling with us, has taken ill. We ask you kindly to be calm. If there is a doctor present, we ask him to come forward." But there was no doctor on board.

Talya could not avoid glimpsing the taint of a smile of satisfaction on Bartholomew Free's lips.

Later, when they landed, she learned the truth about the Ambassador, that he had died.

That afternoon, she was given the letter to deliver to Ben Ford. The meeting was held in the room at Free's hotel. It seemed to be contrary to the precaution that was usually taken, and she braced for the worst.

"You charming girl," Bartholomew Free greeted her, his teeth showing under an arch of grinning lips. "You shall be commended for your excellent work. You have served."

She entered and sat down at his beckoning, noticing the obvious preparations he had made, the two glasses, the champagne, and the pewter bucket with ice. His manner was precise to accompany the care he had taken. And he apparently had just bathed and shaved, the odor of cologne pervading the room. She felt an overwhelming repulsion as he drew close, fingering the two letters he held in his hand.

"We intercepted these from the Philippine representative to the UN, Sebastian Giorgio. The late Ambassador Pope considered himself exceedingly clever." He groaned, "Not so clever, Talya, that he could fool me. It was that moment the Ambassador passed the two letters to the

Filipino. Now we scooped him up and he's peaceful under the influence of drugs. We'll keep his disappearance to ourselves. It is important. Realization that he has disappeared could conceivably delay our plans. We do not want to eliminate him as yet; he may have further value."

The girl listened impassively, it appeared, but the cunning of Operation Baffle intrigued her, if only the information could be used as a counterstroke for the release of her brother, Carlo.

"The Ambassador learned practically all from that double agent in Saigon. It's evident from this first letter. The other is a dupe which Giorgio was to release in the event he was seized, you shall now deliver to Mr. Ben Ford."

She felt it was wise to speak and not display a complete disinterest. "What shall happen to the traitor in Saigon?"

Free indicated by drawing a finger across his throat. "What else? It's too good for him."

She concealed her hatred for the man before her.

"Now I'll put this letter in its envelope, and you shall be off to Mr. Ford with the dupe. The other, Stavros will want to see."

Talya was relieved that possibly the conversation was over and she could depart, despite the fact she would have liked to learn more of Operation Baffle.

"A toast to our success, Talya," Free spoke softly, and thrust a filled glass of champagne before her. She saw it would be hazardous to refuse, and accepted it. They both drank, he quickly and with a heated anxiety, she slowly and coldly, setting the drink aside.

"Talya," he began, "you are beautiful, you are, I must, I must."

He was trembling with excitement so that she feared for her life because of the look in his face.

"No, please, no," she spoke, thrusting out her hand.

And seeing that she would not succumb to his pressure,

Bartholomew Free's mind grasped for the one thing Talya could not resist.

"Remember Carlo, Talya," he said. "I am no less powerful in this consideration than Stavros."

It was possible that, at that point, Talya, against better judgment, would have struck a blade to his heart if a knife were placed in her hand. But she had learned the futility of resistance when the life and love of her brother might be lost.

She swore vengeance on Bartholomew Free.

These thoughts consumed her as she waited in the Hayden for her signal to leave for the waterfront.

If only now, she thought to herself, I could see Ben Ford. I could help him. For I know what he wants to know. The time, the places, the names and what would happen. For when Free was called away, I was able to copy the letter that he had forgotten upon the table. And thus, they might be repaid–but it must be with the protection of Carlo; then may I avenge myself with the exposure of Operation Baffle.

"Was it now possible to like a man this quickly?" was the thought in Talya's mind.

It was just a meeting, a brief meeting, but in Ben she saw something which caused her feelings to show and her heart to go out to him.

It was an impossible situation. She could do little to lessen her pain.

When she was a schoolgirl in Honolulu she read about and saw in the theatres the fanciful land of the supremely happy American–at least, she seemed at that adolescent age to remember only those more glorified pictures. When she developed into a more womanly person, she realized things were much different than she imagined.

Now, as she remembered Ben, she felt that here, perhaps, was the different kind–someone she could desire and love. Why she should so be attracted to this one man, she did not know. She felt she saw an innate goodness in him that she failed to note in many others.

And when Carlo, her brother, was seized by Stavros her world crumbled and fell to pieces. More than anything else in the world, she needed someone she could place trust in.

She was caught up in a hell, a hell she was forced to live with, a manmade hell that was the makings of Stavros and Free.

If only Ben realized her full intent that night. It was impossible to speak over the phone. She feared for Carlo's sake. But Ben could not know.

She felt the sorrow of the impression she must have given him. All seemed unimportant compared to the disasters that Stavros was plotting. It seemed an impossible, fictitious matter. Somehow, some way, she must find a means to notify Ben. A message, perhaps, could be left at the desk for Ben. Something that only he would understand if it were intercepted. Then he would find her and she could explain.

She feared for her brother. And this alone prevented her from exposing Free and his kind.

The shrill ring of the phone startled her from her trance.

It was too late, she thought, to write, and her muddled mind was confounded with fear.

"Who is this?" the voice asked with a sharpness she recognized.

"Talya Laylo," she replied softly through her bloodless lips.

"Okay," the voice replied curtly. "We are waiting."

The devil is waiting, she thought, the devil in all horror and despicableness. I go to meet the devil and my continuing despair.

The room was a swirl of lights and colors. She sunk to the sofa for a moment and steadied herself. She stood up and went to pick up her coat.

With a last glance about the room, and once more the thought of Ben Ford before her, she departed. The clerk at the desk was kind but Talya said nothing. When she reached the street, she knew someone was following her. But, as luck would have it, the fog rolled in from the sea. The pursuing man would have great difficulty in following her taxi. The streets seemed cold and unfriendly; she knew this was in her mind, that this was her despair. Then the waterfront, the departure of the taxi which she followed with her eyes, a last recollection of San Francisco and Ben Ford. The red taillight disappeared in the night.

"Come quickly," a voice behind her beckoned, and she followed rapidly to the pier and the hard, salt-sprayed wooden steps that led down to the chugging boat. There was a screech of tires from where she had walked a few seconds before. The boat pulled away and nothing sounded but the splashing of the water, and then came the enveloping darkness of the night and fog.

Finally they were at a yacht's side. The click of her leather heels sounded on metal. It was cold. She shivered. She entered above and the yacht carefully moved from the boat, traveled a short distance westward, and disappeared on the waters of the Pacific.

Seven

THE HEAVY PEDESTRIAN TRAFFIC clogged the sidewalks of Manhattan. It was a warm sunlit afternoon with a forecast of thunderstorms for the evening. The rain would alleviate the water shortage and the heat.

As planned, Ben and Gumper met at a restaurant in Times Square. The area had changed somewhat, but it was still the center of bustling humanity to Ben.

Gumper showed his confidence. "We checked the passenger list as you suggested, and the whereabouts of each person who traveled with Ambassador Pope. Of course, we can account for Miss Laylo and Free. That left the others." He sipped on a steaming cup of coffee. "We could account for everyone and we checked them all."

"Great," Ben said, expressing a gloomy conclusion to this particular avenue of investigation.

"There was one catch, though," Gumper continued. "It was this rep from the Philippines, supposed to have arrived at their United Nations Headquarters. Sebastian Giorgio. When we checked his office, they said he called to say he was detained in San Francisco. They said he did not elaborate, something about the Ambassador Pope affair—and would be along later. When we tried to trace him in San Francisco, we couldn't get any further line on him. Except a funny thing; he hadn't checked out of his hotel and his bill was paid in advance–to last night."

"Interesting," Ben said. "This could prove extremely valuable. On the other hand, he could be off on a spree some place and show up shortly to resume his work."

"It would have to be today. This would be the day for him to check out."

"Unless he prolongs it."

"True, though it doesn't seem reasonable." Gumper continued, "The important additional bit of information was that he was very well known to Ambassador Pope. But get this, when we checked the hostess and a few others on the trip, they were not aware of any particular friendship between the two. What ideas does that give you?"

Ben's eyes flickered. "Just one, and the one you're thinking about. Ambassador Pope could possibly have entrusted information to Mr. Giorgio."

"And to go further," Gumper put in, "if this is a fact, he was intercepted before he could relay the information to you or the State Department in San Francisco."

"Now we have poor Giorgio in a hell of a mess."

"If only we had grabbed Talya Laylo, we might have cracked this case."

Ben shifted uneasily. "That, I am afraid, is impossible. She has left as quickly as she arrived." He leaned forward.

"There is a suspicion in my mind now that she might have wanted to tell me more, you know, to come to her room."

"I sympathize with you."

"What do you suggest?" Ben asked.

"This, Ben." Gumper laid his hand upon the table. "We let Talya Laylo slip out of our grasp. The only one we have now as a lead, and at the moment he seems above suspicion, is

Bartholomew Free. I don't quite figure his place in the Catskills; I think it needs a going over. We should check it out."

"What do you suggest?" Ben asked, in an obvious feeling of curiosity. "You can't very well barge in—not without some warrant. And the police would have to come in on that; obtain the warrant."

"I know, but why should we get involved in that problem?" This was not according to the book, Gumper knew. Someone would have to explain to him how the rights of an individual should be protected, when, say, in a case of this sort, the worst could be in the works to happen. Gumper was an upholder of the law, the rights of the individual, but, at times, he felt the problems it presented–the not being able to take the needed action because of a law that might delay it. Anyway, he suggested mildly, "Tonight, when it's dark. It will give us some cover and we can look around."

Ben could imagine the Indian territory along Barrymore–what he had read in countless tales. He saw small images of the Halloween night, the triangular eyes and sharp–pointed teeth of the pale orange pumpkin, the frightened black cat on a limb of a tree with its tail sharply inclined to the frozen faced moon in the pitch black sky, and the witch with pointed cap and Colonial days broom passing in the distance along the beams of the reflecting satellite. That was what he imagined about a trip to the Catskills, but it was nothing too much like that.

That evening on the ride, he recalled Regina's farewell. When he might see her again was left uncertain. He said nothing to Gumper, whose concentration seemed elsewhere and on the white lines that separated the traffic.

Ben had been intrigued by her recounting of the Crown of St. Stephen. What part that could play in his plans, he did not know. This was the Crown that was very important to the people of Hungary. It was strange how the faith of a people could rely so strongly on this Crown. And yet, it seemed true. He could not speak to Regina this way; he feared that it would upset her. Since the time the Crown was lost, Hungary seemed beset with a multitude of problems. Perhaps, it would have been best, Ben reflected, if the Allies had returned the Crown.

But to think of those awful difficult times. It was easy now to say return it. Men of Hungary had risked their lives to protect it, to seal and store, then to turn it over to the Americans for their safekeeping.

This was a quandary for Ben. Should he wish and hope for Regina's success–that she might prevail for the successful return of the Crown? Her ideology was different than his. She represented a foreign country, a Communist world. This was not his world. And he would not be the hypocrite to say there was no difference. He was fighting that world. Had not Ben just recently fought in San Francisco against the Agent Koslow? Okay, so he knew spying went on both sides, but that did not mean there could be an acceptance of their ways by Ben. The cold calculated war went on with only an occasional thaw. As long as it stayed that way, it was livable, and in some considerations, the competition was not bad.

Ben and Gumper left Manhattan in a rented Chevrolet and gunned their way up to Barrymore. The highway was excellent driving and they made good time until they were about twenty miles from Barrymore and needed to cut off onto a secondary road.

It began to rain, just a few drops foretelling what was predicted for the evening. At Barrymore, they alighted short of their destination, and, dressed as vacationers, hiked the balance of the distance to Benton Road, stopping occasionally to check their approach and position. Gumper led a circuitous route which would bring them upon a byway leading behind the rear of the farmhouse. They walked steadily the last few minutes until the rear of the farmhouse, silhouetted against the darkening sky, appeared before them. Within a few minutes, the evening shadows filled and blackness prevailed. They moved stealthily through some thickets and brush to a point approximately ten feet behind an abandoned barn which stood sturdily.

They waited, checking behind, convinced they had aroused no suspicions, and then made a study of their position and the surroundings. Two cars stood in the driveway, one Gumper could identify as Free's Mercedes, the other was a new, black Continental. He had never seen it before.

Some lights showed through on the sides of shades which were drawn down. In the upstairs rooms, the windows were open. Sheer lace curtains splashed through to the outside, caught in the crosscurrent of the breeze within the house. The sky darkened severely from the cumulonimbus clouds that drifted over.

Gumper swore because it meant the rain might be heavy. He signaled Ben and they moved across to the rear of the house and beneath a porch that appeared infrequently used.

"You know, we could look pretty damned stupid," Ben whispered, "if this place turns out to be a rest home or something equally unimportant to us."

"I doubt it."

They heard voices, men's voices, heavy and businesslike. They waited a while. Ben motioned to the open window above but Gumper waved him off.

Ben said: "I don't mean to go in. Just to listen. It may help."

Gumper offered his folded hands as a step. Grasping the side of the porch, and with the support from Gumper, Ben felt himself thrust upward. He hoisted himself upon the roof of the porch and paused.

A slash of lightning lit the sky; a clap of thunder followed. Almost in the same instant that the thunder rolled, the rear door of the house was opened. It was off to the left, their view obscured by a cluster of lilac bushes. They could see the top of the screen door open, the spring that held it stretching, and heard the screen slam back into its jambs.

The back of a thin, hastily dressed man appeared. He walked to the Continental, slid into the driver's seat and started the engine. Gunning it several times, he left the car idling, and returned to the farmhouse.

It was then that Ben stuck his head into the room which was dark and its contents blurredly outlined. His eyes adjusted to the darkness, and he could distinguish a bed, an old-fashioned bureau, and wicker chairs. The room was uninhabited.

On the further side, the door to the room was open and he heard voices. They were the voices of men, three men, and it struck him strangely that the one voice seemed familiar to him.

"The car is ready," the words sounded above the others nervously. "Is he ready?"

The answer came back with authority, "Let us leave then for Montauk."

It was the rain slick slate, a tile roof, that did it. Ben lifted his position slightly and, thereafter, was unable to check himself. He began to slide and turn; he was falling to what he felt was certain disaster. He tried to catch the edge of the roof but this availed him nothing. He fell solidly on the stairs, splintering its railing and, as luck would have it, sent a scramble of pails reverberating through the night.

Shouting broke out inside the farmhouse. The lights were doused, and figures began to emerge from the side door again.

"Quickly, quickly," someone spoke. "Let's go!"

Their excitement was evident.

The outline of the thin man emerged again, and along with another burly individual, they walked hastily supporting another man between them. They were heading for the car.

Ben saw Gumper make his move to stop them. Shaking the cobwebs out of his dazed head, Ben lifted himself on his elbow and, at this action, he spied the small figure of Bartholomew Free at the arch of the porch door, a gun in his hand.

"Watch it, Gump," Ben shouted, rolling and concealing himself along the porch. "The bugger's got a gun."

This caused Gump to turn his gaze towards Free. He fell, a wrestler's fall, with quick reaction, a .38 sprouting from beneath his jacket. The maneuver was not entirely successful. Free pumped his gun quickly in the darkness; three shots and one found its mark in Gumper's shoulder. Gump returned the fire, but Bartholomew Free eluded his aim. The Continental roared away towards the highway; the Mercedes lay silently behind.

It was a bad time for Ben and Gumper; still, they were on their feet again. Gumper was holding his right hand to his left shoulder.

"How bad is it?" Ben asked.

"It's okay, let's move. Our car's too far away. Maybe we can find the keys to the Mercedes inside."

They proceeded cautiously into the farmhouse, and Ben snapped on the lights.

A red smear of blood showed on Gumper's jacket and between his fingers.

The room was dimly lit, but they saw the complete abandonment. Nothing was left behind. It was evident that Free and the others were just in the process of leaving. The chair in which they held their prisoner was broken, and abrasions showed where the handcuffs had been attached.

"Nothing," Gumper said. "We were just not in time."

"He mentioned Montauk. One of them said Montauk."

"Where the hell is that?" Gumper asked.

"The tip of Long Island. I've sailed that way."

"It's too late to make it to our car," Gump said, wincing from the slug in his arm. "They left nothing behind."

Ben scooted through the farmhouse, flicking on lights and searching to no avail. He found little and nothing of value.

They walked outside, along the dirt driveway where the Continental had been parked. It was very dark, yet Ben knew he stepped on a foreign object. He felt down and picked up a glove of soft suede, commonly used for driving. It must have fallen out from the side of the Continental. The Mercedes lay like a silent cat in the darkness. Ben opened its door, the lights blinking on and peered down at the glove.

"Strange," he spoke to Gumper who had followed him. "It's a glove for a right hand. Must have been used for driving. But the odd part is, it has only the thumb and three fingers. Look, no spot for a little finger."

"Maybe it's not human," Gumper said, but he could not laugh. The pain was extreme and he wanted to tell Ben about it.

In a length of time that seemed an eternity to Gumper, they made it back to their car. It was a short ride to the center of Barrymore and to a Dr. Hyde who looked upon the two visitors at first as hoodlums up from the big city. This matter was straightened out without too much difficulty.

Ben got on the phone to Washington, and, after a short delay, located Mark Crescent.

"We have to intercept them off Montauk. They have a head start, but it's worth a try. I'll call the Coast Guard from here," Mark said.

The following morning it was reported in a local newspaper, a Continental was abandoned in a sandy spot near Montauk. What happened to the occupants was unknown. A strange aspect of the story seemed to be the many male footprints that led to the water's edge from the car, leading the reporter to believe the occupants boarded a fishing craft of some sort. The further perplexing information was the fact the car had been impounded by the government, the writer suspecting that some sort of illegal smuggling was involved. This still would not explain the abandonment of the lushly equipped vehicle. Not a bit of evidence was left in the car. It was found to be registered to a John Manfred, but his whereabouts were unknown.

Actually, John Manfred was upon the waters of the Atlantic, pondering the means by which he and his associates would eventually arrive in Albania and the countryside above Tirana.

Eight

FOR THE NEXT WEEK Gumper was recuperating in a hospital bed. He did not like it, he rebelled, but when he attempted to escape his confinement, he found himself clutching the metal pipe at the foot of the bed for support. During that eventful evening, he had lost much blood with the damaging results having a delayed effect, and appearing in his pallid face the following day.

Ben drove down to Washington where he had been called for a conference by Mark Crescent.

"I heard about what happened, Ben," Clarissa Neale said, hugging him tenderly. She kissed his cheek and began to cry.

"You silly girl," Ben said, and he patted her head which rested against his chest.

"And you don't even carry a gun."

"I'm not supposed to," he said. "And anyway, I'm indestructible. Nothing can happen."

"You say that," she responded, "but you're human, Ben. I'm afraid, always."

He smiled at her concern but that did not reassure her.

Mark Crescent twisted a string about his finger. Fastened to the end of the string was a picture of Talya.

"Not a bad-looking dish," he said.

Ben nodded.

"What's up, Mark? I know you didn't get me in here to show me a picture of Talya Laylo."

Turning his back to Ben, Mark snapped open a cabinet, drew out two glasses and set several bottles of liquor beside them. What was he up to? Ben said, "the same" when Mark asked.

The spirits were set before them. Ben drank and felt the warmth in his throat. He sat back, relaxed.

"You had a tough time up there?"

"It wasn't bad until that Bartholomew Free started firing."

"You both were lucky. That's Gumper's profession, not yours."

"I've been shot at before."

Crescent pushed the glass aside, a determined precise look in his eyes.

"You want to go on?"

"You kidding?" Ben shot back. "Why, what's up?"

"I would have told you, you had to go on, anyway; it's as bad as that," Mark replied. "This is like any guy fighting up in the front line doing his job. When they took pot shots at you that was only a declaration of a hot war. Operation Baffle is big, and we've got to stop it. We can't, though, unless we find out what the hell it's all about."

His hand slapped hard on the desk.

"We've lost two of our biggest opportunities when we let the girl and Free get away. We don't know where Free is, but we can guess he has landed some place off the Coast of Africa, with the rest of the combine. We know the girl was landed there and flown to Albania."

"Albania?" Ben quizzed.

"Right. This has been confirmed very well through operatives. Actually, it can be said we worked backwards. An operative tipped us off about her landing in Albania. It was almost through a mistake because we were checking on the arrival of some foreign technicians in Albania. Then, working from that point, we were able to determine the flight she came in on, its departure point in Africa, and some astounding maneuvers that occurred about the Coast of Africa in that area at that time. We figure the same for the rest of them you ran into at Barrymore. The tough part is, it looks like they've taken this Sebastian Giorgio with them. They apparently are not certain how much he knows and are holding him as insurance.

"Ben," Crescent spoke with the greatest seriousness, "we are going to send you to Rome temporarily to await further instructions. When they do come, you will be given the greatest assignment of your life. We expect to place you in Albania in the care of one of our agents. After which you will contact Talya Laylo. We feel she can help us, possibly reveal enough information that we can stop Operation Baffle dead in its tracks."

"But why should she help me? Or us?" Ben questioned. "She's probably as deadly as the rest."

"I doubt it," Mark replied. "You see, we checked her background. There was one link we caught on to. She had a brother in Indonesia. His name was Carlo Laylo. When we traced it through we found he had been kidnapped and used as a pawn to work against her. We further found by counterwork that she was never involved before in any foreign politics, subversive work, or the like. They dragged her into it since she was an entertainer and in a position to help them."

"So how does that leave us, Mark?"

Crescent stood up and faced away, looking out the window, his back to Ben Ford. When the words came, they resounded from the wall like a recording somewhere in the room because Ben could not see his lips move.

"He's dead, Ben. Been shot trying to give them the slip." He turned slowly, his hands folded behind his back and faced Ford again, his voice unchanging and calm. "That's why we have to work fast. Her days may be numbered. If she gets word what has happened or they figure she's no use anymore, bingo, they'll eliminate her."

"The buggers," Ben muttered. He tapped his glass and Mark continued to pour. It was strong, good stuff; Ben needed it.

"I suppose you want me to get the message to her and you figure she'll break."

"That's about it."

"But why can't your agent do it just as well?"

"It's possible, but she might not believe him. It would be a chance, and if it failed, we'd be done. No. She might tip the whole thing and ruin everyone. She knows you and we are of the opinion she will trust you."

For a while a distinct pause ensued. The slight noise of the business day came through from outside. The sound of Clarissa Neale's typing could be heard. Ben mulled over what he had learned.

"When do I leave?" Ben asked.

"In three hours for Rome."

Clarissa kissed him when he was departing. She knew something dangerous was brewing.

For the first time Ben thought of her differently. In the past, he knew he had teased her and joked with her as if she were always there, part of the room. Now he realized she was dead serious, sensitive and very concerned. Her button eyes were full of tears. It added up to something painful. She could not conceal she loved him. The difference was while he could treat her kindly, he was not in love with her.

The Hotel King Roma was a most exquisite and

fashionable hotel. The one thing that intrigued Ben was that the customers, with the exception of the obvious quickly moving foreign transient trade, were all cut to specification. Some politicians resided there, people in foreign offices, entertainers, and fast paced jet sets with substantial silver and gold deposits backing their pursuits.

The Roman sky was always clear and beautiful, the days extremely hot, but Ben was fortunate to enjoy a few cool evenings. While he had time, he journeyed to Ostia for a swim, he shopped along the Via Veneto, and visited the art galleries and ancient buildings of which there were many to enjoy.

When the men with the ice cream came by, he would buy at any price and stroll casually, his jacket draped over his arm, through the streets of the city.

It was during one of these strolls that he found his great discovery and joy.

At first, he could hardly believe his eyes, but, before him, in all her loveliness, was Regina. She was wearing dark glasses so that, even as she looked in his direction, she failed to recognize Ben Ford.

"Regina!" he called. Her face was turned slightly away from him, but the sound of her name being spoken brought recognition. "My good Lord!" she exclaimed, and removing her glasses, gazed happily at him. "Ben Ford."

She seemed strangely embarrassed. The initial hesitancy vanished. She cried, "Ben!" and was lost in the crush of his arms around her.

The few people and passersby in the street tittered and smiled at them.

Ben noticed the awkwardness of their situation. Drawing Regina close to his side, they walked together a short distance to where a table was empty at a sidewalk cafe.

Ben swept her up; it seemed unfair, he reflected

afterwards. She was given so little time to think. It seemed he possessed her, and she had no opportunity to object, or protest. This was the wonder of it all. She fell in with his desires and happiness, and her depth of feeling made her abandon the lesser plans of the day.

"To find you in Rome, so quickly, so soon," Ben said. "This is a cause for celebration. Never would I have expected to see you here. I'm sure I would not have wasted so much time in getting here."

They rode in a small borrowed car along the outskirts of Rome and to the seaside.

At one point along the countryside, they were forced to stop when a bearded farmer, along with a young lad of around twelve, guided some cattle to a pasture that lay green and cool and inviting.

The farmer, who was a friendly elderly man, recognized the foreign appearances of the couple. Regina's long golden hair that swept along her shoulders or perhaps the somewhat American dress of Ben may have given him cause to think so.

"Not long ago," he said, "a mine, maybe an old bomb from a plane, I am not too sure, exploded while the animals were grazing." The farmer waved his hand in the direction of the greenness of the field. "Probably a German mine, I am not sure; I don't think it was from the planes. Pietro thinks so. I don't." He shook his head. "Anyway, it makes me worry. I don't like to take the cows there to feed because of what happened. I guess that is why there is so much to feed on in that part."

Regina listened with an obviously deep intentness that seemed unusual. Her interest, Ben imagined, was from the experiences in her own land. Ben recalled that his earlier years in Ohio did not present such concerns; he led a fairly secure and free life in his youth. Her sincere interest in the problem of this man struck Ben. It was comforting to see the keen interest a person might have in the problems of others. He saw this in

Regina.

The Crown of St. Stephen's interested her deeply because it contained something important of the past for many people in Hungary.

"You are new married couple?" the farmer asked while directing the lightly clothed lad to lift away the log that acted as a gate and a barrier.

A slight embarrassment tinged Regina's face.

"Not yet," Ben replied.

"You make a fine couple," the farmer continued, "and I wish you the best of luck and happiness." He was not to be swayed from his impression of the pleasantness of the couple.

"Do you think he was right?" Ben asked as they got their car started again along the narrow paved road.

"What is that?" Regina asked coyly. She knew what Ben was referring to, but on this occasion would not give an answer which might reflect her concern and thoughts.

"He was ready to pronounce us man and wife. Do you think he was right?"

Regina pushed him on the shoulder with a pretended disgust at his frankness.

"You are unkind sometimes, Ben," she protested. And she was momentarily scared, placing her hands to her lips, when Ben faked a temporary loss of control of the car because of her thrust at his shoulder.

When she clutched him timidly, he said: "You see what I mean, you love me; it is quite obvious."

"You know nothing of me. It is so quick what has happened. Should you wait a while before considering such an important step?"

"Did I tell you I love you, Regina?"

"Yes, many times; almost the first night we met."

"When Mr. Bancroft introduced us."

She withdrew slightly from Ben.

"What's the matter?" Ben asked.

"Have you heard," she said quickly, "that he has come to Rome?"

"No," Ben replied. "What for?"

"Not that I am sure, but he did mention he was coming. Did he not say the same to you?"

"Hardly," Ben replied, "I met him only that evening."

Regina was hesitant to speak further on the matter and Myles Bancroft held no particular interest for Ben.

Nine

BEN AND REGINA SPENT the next three days together.

One evening they found a small, quaint restaurant where they could dine and talk. It was away from the usual thoroughfares. The food was good, inexpensive, and delightfully spicy. The red Chianti was heavy and strong. Ben wanted it this way. He did not want to be fussed about. It was his desire to relax and enjoy the wonderful atmosphere, the climate, the sun, the occasional shade of an arbor, and the slow tempo of the day with Regina.

He looked at the wine, raising his glass up to the light so that the rays sparkled through. He was aware of the warmth of this wine and the stimulation it gave him.

The following morning, they traveled to Como with the intention of returning the next day. Ben left word how he might be reached. He deliberated before leaving whether this was right to do and that possibly an urgent call might come in for him to hurry off. These were not his instructions, he recalled.

He had been told to hold and wait.

Ben enjoyed the feel of the Ferrari and felt invigorated at the end of the drive. It seemed impossible that he was not fatigued.

They dined, and then left for a chalet one of his friends at the State Department had offered him the use. The water was charmingly beautiful; the movements of the boats along the lake stood out against the background of the Italian landscape.

The dusk of evening settled in, and they waited until the stars of the heaven shone. The air and the night were supremely beautiful.

Regina spoke softly to him. "Ben, I know why you brought me here." He protested, but she closed his lips. "Please, do not say anything. I can understand. I love you, Ben. Please, love me always, Ben."

Their happiness was no less on their return. It seemed an odd request; but Ben stopped the Ferrari along the road for her to get out when she requested it. She wanted to pick some flowers, some white petal daisies that waved from the slight breeze in the field. When Ben followed, she began to run and run and run. Ben ran as fast as he could until he had overtaken her.

"Come on," he shouted happily, having caught her. "There are some things I must learn about you."

She was completely out of breath and collapsed helplessly in his arms.

They were along a slight knoll that overlooked the workers in the fields. The knoll was soft with the greenness of the grass.

Ten

WHEN BEN RETURNED TO the Hotel King Roma that evening, the word had arrived. He called and told Regina he would see her somewhat later; he was sorry he could not dine with her.

There was a noticeable disappointment in her voice.

Ben journeyed over to the State Department office and met with John Sergi, who was an American agent working in Rome.

Sergi spoke clipped, distinctly. He was extremely careful, ever checking parts of the room they were in, despite the fact it was American property.

"You leave tonight, Ben. What the heck happened? We were looking for you. We got your message but figured you'd be back earlier." He mopped his brow with a white, tightly folded handkerchief. He listened to Ben's quick explanation, then continued, "You'll take these old clothes and put them on before you board the boat at Brindisi. The ride over may be a little rough because of some thunderstorms predicted, but it should be smooth when you reach the coast of Albania. You carry no identification. If anything should happen after you've been turned over to our agent and you should be apprehended, just say nothing and hold tight." There were further explanations and cautions; Ben knew this was repetitious, for repetition's sake, having been fully briefed a few days before. Sergi ended off by giving the name of Ben's contact. "Coranis. He will take you to the girl and back to our rendezvous for your return to this country."

Ben inspected the clothing. He knew they would fit because Sergi ordered them tailored for him. They would blend in with the general dress of the area. Olive brown coarse woolen trousers, heavy leather shoes, a dark plaid shirt, and a cap, weather-beaten, as one might expect fishermen to wear. The pipe posed no problem; he loved to smoke a pipe. But, here again, Sergi provided him with a pipe and tobacco from that area Ben was invading.

"Coranis speaks excellent English. There will be no problem," Sergi spoke. "You will learn something of Coranis when you meet him and spend your time with him. He is highly dependable. We are fortunate here." The concern was in Sergi's face, the concern that all was properly prepared. Sergi's way was to worry about the least item, aware that the slightest error could jeopardize the operation and lead to misfortune. In a matter of this sort, if all is properly checked, he knew, at least to the extent that human care and effort allowed, the chances of success were good. As long as everyone did his part.

"You will find Coranis an agreeable, friendly man. Sometimes, I wonder why. He has experienced so many heartaches. Lost his wife and child during the war. He was a guerilla during the last war and there were many hardships, believe me, during those times. I don't think he or the Italian soldiers who went to fight knew what it was all about. And then the Germans. Coranis saw much trouble there. Living under the constant chase with no special equipment. Lack of food, in some instances. And the suffering of the people. The hell of the war."

Sergi stood up, indicating he was finished with his

briefing. "A car will pick you up at your hotel in two hours. You will please be ready promptly, Ben. I know this leaves you little time. You may not have the amount of time you wish to have to say goodbye to anyone."

Sergi's poker face did not reveal what he was thinking.

"You have met the driver," he continued. "He will bring you to your plane and you should be in Brindisi sometime later tonight. From there, you shall receive transportation to the boat."

Sergi extended his hand.

"I wish you the greatest luck, Ben. And I look forward to your safe and successful return."

Ben found Regina at her hotel. She said she was feeling fine, but Ben sincerely doubted her assurances. Her eyes were troubled although she made some attempt to cover her feelings.

"What's this all about?" he asked.

"I fear losing you again."

"But it is only a few days."

"You say that, Ben," she replied. "But I know you are undertaking something dangerous. You have never mentioned it once. Even as you started to speak before, you hesitated and I could tell by your expression your concern."

He did realize the danger in his confrontation with Operation Baffle. They murdered Joshua Pope, they murdered in the outskirts of Saigon. He wondered where their killings ended. And Bartholomew Free had fired his gun at him and Gumper.

Now, as he stood with Regina, the first concern of his safety came sharply to him. He feared this experience, the thought he would become concerned about fear. Before, without Regina, his personal safety seemed less important, but with her before him and the glorious memory of their relationship revolving in his mind, he found for an instant, a different thought. Will I be okay, or will it end here, this last look at her before I depart?

Ben wondered why she must worry so. In his care to conceal his assignment, perhaps he became too careful and unintentionally revealed in his demeanor and speech something of the secret–the concern of his mission into Albania.

In this last moment then, before his departure, with the words of Sergi in his thoughts that he must not delay, he bent forward and kissed her.

"Do not worry for me, Regina," he assured her. "It is nothing, I tell you. I love you now. I shall love you always.

"You will wait for me, Regina? I shall see you again," he said.

She trembled and her body became limp; a deep somber fear enveloped her.

"I shall see you, Ben. I shall love you forever."

On his way back to his hotel, Ben found something foreign in his pocket. It was a beautiful red rose, just blooming from its newness.

He smiled and smelled its fragrance.

Eleven

BEN WOULD NEVER FORGET the run over from Brindisi.

As Sergi informed, they ran into some squally weather and were pelted with rain and hailstones. The seas were high and choppy; the lightning slashed the night and the thunder rolled above their heads. But as suddenly as the onslaught had come, as quickly it disappeared, and they found themselves in relatively calm seas.

The captain and crew had made the trip many times and were familiar with the waters as they were their own names.

After some time, they were riding off the coast of Albania, proceeding slowly and carefully. Every light was out on the boat as the atmosphere became more tense and the danger zone drew nearer. The captain explained that they were on radar. They were concerned with other crafts that might be nearby, and the Albanian boats that served as their Coast Guard. The land was a dim, long shadow in the distance, with an occasional light or cluster of lights blinking from the villages. It was very quiet now and Ben imagined the towns were buttoned up.

The captain of the boat, he was called Pesce, was an old

individual whose face looked like leather when Ben studied him earlier under the artificial lights and whose hands were large and distorted, Ben thought, from the endless lifelong chores on the sea. This was no slacker's paradise; the life on the water offered as much as was given.

The stem of the corncob pipe was gripped in Pesce's teeth and the smoke swirled backward towards the stern of the boat. Along the rail he stopped a while to chat with Ben, apparently figuring the American was feeling the uneasiness of the approaching day in a strange country, in a strange, almost hostile environment.

"We have to watch for boats carefully," he spoke in a harsh voice with a noticeable accent. It was the accent of the Southeastern region of Italy, mellow and firm. "Lots of illegal trade. They come from North there," and he pointed with the stem of his pipe towards the coast. "Sometimes, they get caught. Then it's bad. Lose their boat. They have much trouble."

Ben followed the mysterious black lines of the coast and Pesce's conversation. He did feel some uneasiness; his hands, however, were steady and his thinking clear and methodical as it should be. Once ashore he knew the time would pass swiftly and he would have little opportunity for useless worries.

"You like this sort of thing?" Pesce asked.

"It's my job," Ben replied.

"I take these chances but I'm used to them now," Pesce continued. "When the Germans come in the big war, I lost my boat. But afterwards, when the Americans throw them out, I got my boat back. And then I helped the Americans. I help them again. I'll never forget they gave me my boat back."

It was as simple as that. Pesce became a devoted friend to the Americans because they returned his life to him, as represented by the solid frame and hull and cabin of a fishing boat.

"Are you scared?" Pesce asked.

"Let's say I'm concerned," Ben replied.

"You have a gun?"

"No," Ben replied. "I don't believe in carrying one. If I get into trouble, I'll have to dig myself out somehow."

Pesce grinned, "Well, you are brave, but it is better to have a gun."

The smell of the salt sea permeated the air. Ben felt the dampness about him. It was good that the clothes he was wearing were wool. His body was warm.

"This government thinks big of the communists. You better be careful," Pesce said, pointing straight to the land mass beyond.

"I'll keep that in mind," Ben laughed.

"The Americans are fighting there now. I knew they would. I don't care what you call it, what is going on now they are fighting the others." Pesce appeared current with world affairs. Life on the sea gave him time to read and cogitate.

"That's why all our work is important."

"How is that?" Pesce asked.

"We all have to play our part. This fight is not an easy one," Ben replied. "When I think of one American, or anyone else taking it on the chin for me in some line of defense, I can't take it here in the stomach."

Pesce plugged his thumb over the bowl of his pipe; he wanted the fire to go out. "That's the way I feel. That is why I am here." He slapped Ben on the back in a friendly fashion. "The night is damp and cold. I will give you some brandy. Come. We will be at our destination shortly."

Ben followed him to where Pesce took back the navigation of the boat. One of his men brought up some glasses and a new bottle of Martel. They toasted and drank together. Ben appreciated the captain's consideration and thanked him.

"It is nothing," Pesce shrugged. "One thing I know, that you would do the same for me. I remember the Americans with their jokes, but they were always kind."

The sound of the churning motor was lowered when they turned in close to the land and along a promontory which revealed a quiet, peaceful inlet. Ben could hear the slosh of the water along the sides of the hull and the ripple of the Adriatic along the closely lying shore. The features of the land were not fully discernible; Ben could make out there was a smooth length of beach that extended inland about thirty to forty feet to a continuous cliff which rose again about thirty to forty feet above the shoreline. Here and there, rocky projections appeared, or the outlines of scrubby, weather-beaten trees. It was a very quiet scene. The area was obviously uninhabited. Not even the boats which had occasionally appeared earlier were seen.

Pesce struck a line slightly away from the shore with at times a bit of zigzagging to avoid some obstacle or shallowness his long experience had made him aware of.

"It is not bad," he said to Ben, "but it pays to be careful and not argue with your better judgment."

A short ways further, a small light reflected at a point, a sheltered cove. Pesce navigated well, and they were on their target. His abilities in the blackness were uncanny; he expressed his satisfaction on the successful trip.

The light was so situated that it could be seen only from the angle of their approach. If they moved further in or out from shore, the light would have been concealed by the mounds of earth that lay to each side.

Then they traveled sufficiently close that the errant rays of the guiding light seemed to come together and it was visible that it was a storm lamp. In the far reaches of the cliff, a figure moved stealthily along to their destined point. The image was a blur but, as it approached, Ben saw it was a man dressed somewhat as himself; he knew this man was Coranis, his contact.

Methodically Coranis brought a boat from out of the gloom, and paddled carefully, almost noiselessly, towards them. Pesce cut the motor so that the only sound that could be heard was the sound of the moving sea and Coranis' paddle as it struck the water.

"Good luck, my friend," Pesce spoke, and shook Ben's hand warmly. "I wish you the best and a safe return. Coranis will let us know. We will fulfill any plans they decide upon."

Ben thanked him and slid down onto the side of the boat and sat back on the cold, damp wood.

"Mr. Ford," Coranis spoke. "Ben Ford, I am glad to know you."

"And I'm glad to know you, Coranis."

Ben knew his entire success would rest on this man as their hands clasped. He waved to Pesce, who already began to withdraw into the murkiness. The beacon light on shore was extinguished by Coranis. In the distance, the Albatross of Captain Pesce faded to a shadow and finally disappeared back to the open sea.

Ben assisted Coranis in beaching the boat and concealing it along the side of a mound which was thick with brush and brambles. Then they set off together along the beach, up from the sand, however, and over the rocks where their footprints could not appear. Coranis took a little time to cover over the marks of their steps and the keel of the boat that had imprinted the sand.

They walked quietly for about a quarter hour when Coranis set his sights inland. They climbed the stones and dirt of the jutting cliff and found themselves in some long, sloping fields that stretched upward from the coast. The darkness began to yield now and the first light of day approached. Another quarter hour of walking brought them to a tenant stone house, around which livestock could be found, and the natural aroma of livestock could be smelled.

Coranis made one last glance around at the gray of the day and the surrounding horizon. Far in the distance, the first impressions of the Adriatic could be seen. He pushed the door open, stepped inside, lit a lamp, and asked Ben to follow.

"Sit down," Coranis offered.

For the first time, Ben was able to observe Coranis in the light. He was a strikingly hard looking man with a short beard and mustache tinged with gray. His face was ruddy and strongly masculine.

"Have you slept?" Coranis asked. "You should rest, anyway." He continued without waiting for an answer, shaking out a cot that lay along the wall.

This was to be his bed, Ben realized.

"The girl you want to see is about two miles below us here along the coast. It is a little resort town called Sarka."

Ben sat down on his cot.

"Is she alone?" he asked.

"No, there are some others, some men."

Ben thought these others must be Bartholomew Free and his associates with whom he made his brief encounter.

"They have something like a hundred and fifty foot yacht which it looks maybe they use as a fortress. I don't like any of them." Coranis spit on the floor. "Some foreign representatives, too."

"And the girl," Ben asked, "can you tell me anything about her?"

Coranis sat down on his cot at the opposite side of the room; this room served as a bedroom, dining room, and living room. Towards the right rear stood a stone fireplace and storage area for foods; at the left was the lavatory. The dwelling had water facilities, but no other modern lighting and heating conveniences.

Coranis spoke again: "She takes trips always with others as bodyguards. Shopping in the little town and sometimes a trip to Tirana."

"Not too good," Ben suggested, "if we have to go out into the open to see her."

Coranis leaned back on his elbow. "She takes a walk every afternoon, usually after the lunch time. I do not think she will change that."

"Good," Ben responded.

"Not so good," Coranis put in.

"Why?"

"Always this little man follows her."

Ben said, "Bad."

"That is right," Coranis continued. Coranis did not seem desirous of talking about it at any length. "That is one reason why I think she will help you, if she can."

It sounded like Bartholomew Free, who else?—perhaps by some matter regarding her brother, even while Free was undoubtedly aware that he was murdered, and she knew nothing about it. If she would only believe him, Ben could agree with Coranis that Talya would do all to help within her power.

"Do you have any ideas, Coranis, what we can do, how we should plan this, isolate her away from the rest for a while, if possible?"

Coranis' hands were still hard and dirty from the climb and handling of the boat. He rubbed them together as he sat up and pondered.

"I think I have a way. It may be risky. But anything we do will be risky."

Ben asked him to continue.

"This afternoon, if you are ready," Coranis continued, "we go down where we can watch them. I am sure the little man will not fail us. They will be about a mile away from the others in an isolated area. I will draw his attention somehow, do something, and hope he will give chase."

Ben nodded his head. "It may be risky. If it is the little bugger I think he is, he's carrying a gun. And he's already taken aim at me and one of my friends."

"Perhaps. We won't worry." Coranis shrugged it off. "When he follows after me, then your opportunity will come. The girl may be scared and it will be up to you to keep her from trouble. You will have to work out the rest from there."

It was a difficult plan Ben, and no doubt Coranis, realized. Still, if Coranis scouted the girl and the crew as he said he had, there was left really no other avenue of approach to her. Time was also deeply involved here. Operation Baffle, they estimated because of the urgency of Ambassador Pope's information, would not rest and wait in its execution. The fact was that Ben prayed he found sufficient time and that the girl could help them. He dreaded he might hear the news any day that Operation Baffle succeeded and learned his mission failed. He cursed when he thought about it; the waiting in Rome, and how he could have messed up their plans even for a day on his trip away from the city.

"We shall try it," Ben said.

"Then rest now. You will need to be awake and strong."

The last thing Ben recalled was Coranis carefully cleaning his hands as Ben closed his eyes and fell into a deep sleep.

Twelve

BEN HAD WOKE SWEARING and rubbing his eyes. The sound he heard was familiar; it was raining, not the heavy downpour of a passing thunderstorm, but the slow, continuous drizzle of a frontal disturbance. He cursed since it was about noontime, and this would ruin the plan he and Coranis decided upon.

"Never mind," Coranis spoke. "There is tomorrow. The rain will not last."

"But time counts, Ben said. "We may have lost very important time."

"You can do nothing about it." Coranis told Ben he was a Greek and had fought during the last war. He tried to ease the American's anxiety. "Sometimes, when the Fascists come, we are stuck up in the hills for weeks. Nothing to do but wait, always the waiting. It was tough." He rubbed his scraggly beard. "But that is over now. Why talk about it." He clapped his hand and stood up. "You hear of Metaxa. This is not Metaxa. But it is good." Crossing over to Ben, he slapped him on the shoulder. "Come, on, Ben, you and I are going to drink and get stiff, as you say."

They drank and they felt better. It warmed them and

raised their appetite for the coarse, spicy meal Coranis prepared.

At intervals, Coranis searched the surrounding area to see that nothing suspicious was developing; and he needed to tend the livestock. He found a few other small chores to take care of, and spent some time playing cards with Ben. It was mutually agreed that Ben should stay inside and not take any chance of being seen. Occasionally there was a passerby up on the main road which was paved, and some horse drawn carts, speeding cars, and trucks usually carrying farm produce.

After the evening meal, Coranis led Ben to an inner sanctum, a large closet just off the lavatory, which concealed shortwave and radio equipment. He showed him how it was operated, and told him he would have to sit by around eight to check for any reception and information being transmitted to him.

To protect the operation, it was understood that no messages would be transmitted out, but that an operator would be ready to receive at all times across the sea along the Italian coastline, in the event of an emergency.

Later that evening, Coranis displayed a transistor radio and tuned in on a Greek station. He went out of his way to keep Ben occupied, and also to enjoy his temporary companionship.

They awoke the following morning to a beautiful bright day. A little of the dampness of the previous evening was in the air but disappeared when the day grew hotter.

Ben showed some anxiety, but with several glasses of Coranis' liquor, he was his normal self again. He felt wonderful until the time came for them to proceed on their expedition.

Coranis secured the house, checking the few things he had to, and then they started off down towards the beach and short of it turned south along the coast. Before they departed,

Coranis packed a small gun in his pocket and a long hunting knife he attached to his belt.

The route they followed, Coranis figured, would avoid as much contact with others as possible. They did meet a few people; to the ones he knew, Coranis passed a few greetings. He managed to keep Ben away from any conversations.

Actually their journey went smoothly and the last stretch of walking to their destination was deserted and without any incident.

"We shall wait here," Coranis said. They were adequately sheltered and looked down upon a small concealed area.

They rested in the shade of an old oak tree that had shattered some years prior in a storm. Still, it held life and its leaves were hardy and bright. From where they sat, the sea was not far away; the shore was slightly visible along a section of the overhanging cliff which had eroded over a period of time from rainstorms and harsh winters.

Time waiting seemed an eternity, as it always does to the impatient, and Ben became fidgety and impatient. Coranis, who was used to the slow pace of the country, was not bothered. He would rather look at the buzzing insects and the slowly waving high grass of the fields. They felt only a slight breeze that came off the sea.

Coranis motioned Ben to be quiet and set his ears attentively.

"Remember, he cautioned, "when I have distracted him and he follows, this will be your opportunity to gain the attention of the girl and to speak to her. But wait until you are certain that he has followed me. Otherwise, it could be dangerous for you."

Along the shore where the cliff was broken, the figure of Talya Laylo appeared. She was garbed in sport clothes which hung loosely on her frame, somewhat concealing her fine contours. A few paces behind her appeared the small, ruthless Bartholomew Free. Ben recognized him from a picture Gumper had taken of him.

They disappeared briefly and came in sight again over the edge of the cliff that led to the spot Coranis had marked. The couple drew closer so that Ben could see the distraught expression on Talya's face. Free spoke volubly but his words could not be understood at that distance.

Free grasped Talya's arm and she withdrew it harshly, moving away from him.

Ben started up at this, but Coranis restrained him from moving further.

"Wait, Ben, our chance shall come soon."

With that, Coranis moved catlike away from him and quietly southward from Ben.

A short interval passed during which Free continued talking. He was dismayed when the first stone landed nearby. A perplexed look reflected from his face. Gazing around, he saw nothing and was about to shrug it off lightly when another stone struck the ground. Quickly Free moved, striking a direction for the knoll; when he reached the point from where the stones must have been thrown, another stone landed at his feet, thrown from further in the brush and trees. He shot ahead and vanished in pursuit.

It was now Ben's move as he circled down and behind Talya, convinced that Free would be occupied elsewhere for at least some minutes. He came forward and revealed his presence to her.

"Talya, it's me, Ben Ford."

Thank God, she froze, Ben thought. The shriek choked in her throat and she collapsed into his arms. He moved quickly and carried her back again into the field out of sight, and sat down beside her. Ben had gambled. If Free returned, he must think that Talya had become frightened and had run towards the yacht.

When Talya recovered from her faint, Ben covered her

mouth and spoke quickly. "Talya, you must remember me, Ben Ford."

"Yes, yes, Ben," she said, sobbing uncontrollably. Aware again of the dangers of the moment, she stopped.

"Talya, you must believe me. What I am going to tell you is true. Do you understand me? Do you trust me?"

She nodded her head. Her head swirled as if she were in a bad dream. The past year had been a weird dream. She would help Ben Ford. She would steel herself for anything he might wish to say.

Ben lay forward and pressed his cheek to hers. "Please, Talya, be brave. I want to help you." His lips felt her hair that fell about her ear. "Please, Talya, believe what I say, and trust me. I must tell you this," and her sixth sense made her understand before he spoke. "Talya, your brother Carlo is dead. Murdered by those buggers. The nightmare you've endured with those devils is over..."

He felt her body convulse, and heard the sickly coughing sounds she tried to repress. He was forced to lay his cupped hand over her mouth. For those few moments she could think only of Carlo; that he was dead.

"Talya, we do not have time. If they find us here, maybe we would both be shot. I know Free would not hesitate to kill me."

She nodded her head and clutched him tightly. Shortly, her fear passed and a deep unalterable vengeance flashed in her eyes.

"Will you help us, Talya? Can you help us break up this Operation Baffle before it is too late?"

"Ben, I wanted to help you that night in San Francisco. You did not understand me. I was not sure what you were thinking."

She wiped the tears from her eyes.

"Can you help me now?"

"Yes," she replied. "This man, Free, you see what he is.

He had another letter from Ambassador Pope which the Ambassador had given to the Filipino. They have the Filipino on the boat, but they will kill him, Ben. You must save him."

"What is Operation Baffle, Talya?"

"I am not supposed to know, but when this animal, Free, was not aware, I took the letter and wrote down as much as I could in the time I had."

Quickly she removed her right shoe and stocking and brought out from beneath her foot a length of tan adhesive which concealed a paper with minuscule writing.

"It is here. I have written it very small several times. I thought someday to use it to save my brother. But it is too late."

After taking the paper Ben put it deep in his pocket and felt the outside of his trouser to assure its safety.

"It is to happen tomorrow, Thursday, Ben, from the Ambassador Pope's writing. You must act swiftly to prevent what they have planned."

They waited silently in the field now. Ben observed Talya carefully with kindness. She endured so much. He must plan quickly for her, and a course for her to follow.

Peering carefully he sought some sign of the return of Bartholomew Free; there was no sign of him, no activity. The only movement in the sunny afternoon was the flutter of a few birds, the touch of a slight breeze on the tops of high grass, and the occasional turning white caps on the Adriatic. Free followed Coranis deep into the grove.

Talya tightened her hand about Ben's arm. "I cannot endure it now that I know Carlo is dead; I must find a way to destroy them."

"You could start down the beach, Talya, ahead of him. You can say you became frightened and were heading back to the yacht." He ran his hand back over her disheveled hair, and then held her below the chin so that he looked straight down into her eyes. "After we have conveyed this information, we shall find a way to release you tonight. Can you break free of them?"

"It is impossible, Ben. No one is allowed away alone. Even this hour Free was assigned to watch me."

"You remain on the boat?" he asked.

She shook her head. "It is always under guard."

"Quickly, we have little time, Talya. Is there ever a moment when you have some freedom?"

She ran her fingers nervously along the side of her face.

"I don't know, Ben," she hesitated, "unless..."

"Unless what?" Ben asked.

"There is one possibility. When the weather has permitted, in the evening I have taken a swim along the side of the yacht and towards a small raft about a sixty feet away. But I could never get to the land."

"Is the area of the raft lighted?"

"No, but they require me to wear a white bathing suit so I might be more distinguishable."

Ben laid out a plan as quickly as possible and made her repeat it back to him with a special emphasis on the agreed hour of nine-thirty.

"I fear for the Filipino," she said.

"You will have to leave that to me," he said.

They started to move away from their hiding place. Ben used exceptional care to move slowly and not disturb their surroundings. It could be a tip-off to the crafty Free who Ben was certain would momentarily appear. They finally gained a secluded spot along the cliff. After Ben looked back to check for Free's approach, he signaled to Talya, who darted from her position and slid down to the beach and to the point where her and Free's footprints still showed in the sand. She disappeared from his sight.

Ben became quite concerned as he waited for Free's return, and for Coranis. It was impossible to understand all that had happened in the past minutes.

Just as a cloud drifted below the sun and a shadow fell over the hillside, Bartholomew Free burst from the grove. He walked laboriously, his feet leaden until he was at a ridge over the spot where he departed earlier. At that moment, Ben was directly across from him, some hundred feet away, hidden in the flowing field's high grass. Still he could see a look of consternation in Free's face; the little vile man gazed about uncomprehendingly. For a fraction of time, his little face turned to the sky and he seemed to be cursing. He lifted his two hands away from the position he held them on his stomach and thrust them forward for an unseen support. It was then that Ben saw the crimson splash on Free's chest and stomach, the outstretched red-drenched hands, and the trace of blood along the corner of his lips and chin. Bartholomew Free toppled forward and down and down in the yawning, gaping mouth of his hell.

"What did Coranis do? We're in a heck of a spot now!" Ben remembered the paper in his pocket, the scheduled havoc and doomsday date of tomorrow Talya had quickly mentioned, and the task before him. The information must be protected. The gun he swore he must never carry seemed a necessity now. Coranis was nowhere in sight. Ben lunged from his position. He prayed that he would not lose his direction, or be intercepted. Coranis must follow. They agreed that Ben should not wait for him.

Coranis would find his way of making it back.

Thirteen

BEN MADE HIS WAY BACK as swiftly as possible to the Coranis house. His heart pounded heavily. Many lives rested on his capabilities.

Along the way he stumbled and tore his trousers. This could draw people's attention. They would find him a stranger in their territory and in a questionable appearance. From that point on he held along the shore; it would be longer, but he felt it would lead to less suspicion. He rolled his trouser legs up a few turns. Eventually, he would find the bend into the inlet which led up to the area of the farmhouse.

Once, a young girl child saw him as she stood atop the cliff and called to her mother. The woman poked her head over, and shrugged when she saw nothing below. The child was adamant, however, gesturing and speaking in a language unfamiliar to Ben.

"See, see," she seemed to be saying, "he was there. I saw him. He was walking very fast." The young girl would not be denied, tugging at her mother's dress for the woman to follow. It was the slight imprint of Ben's heels that had dug the sand and had broken the continuity of the otherwise undisturbed shoreline. This was what the girl saw and made her insistent despite the protestations of her parent that it was the youngster's imagination.

Ben drew close under the shelter of the cliff and hid himself as best as possible behind some scrub bushes. Beads of sweat covered his forehead; he was almost thankful for the opportunity to rest. The inquisitiveness of the native villagers was not that they were hunting a criminal, but came from a desire to be of assistance. Ben realized this, still mindful of the fact that he wanted no help and simply desired to speed upon his mission unhindered.

Off to the side and southward from his position, Ben saw the youngster and mother reappear, this time accompanied by a robust, weather-beaten man who appeared to be her father. The effort and the search was being taken lightly as a joke and to prove that the imagination sometimes creates strange tricks. What better way was there to make the point clearly except to go right down and investigate? In the meanwhile, Ben was seriously delayed. As great as his purpose might be, he must wait and hope that he was not discovered. After all, he did not know the language. Exactly what his reaction might be depended on their reactions when they glanced at the heel prints.

Slowly, the trio approached the point where Ben had stepped. In close to the cliff, the stones were large and sometimes treacherous. Hand in hand, they made their way down over the rocks. From where Ben watched, the slight breaking of the waves lapped the shore, the edge of the fanning waterline a few feet from his heel prints. As the group drew closer to the spot the girl sought, Ben noticed what seemed a heaven sent white foaming wave roll along the coast and, with its greater momentum, it broke and cast a wave of water flooding high on the beach and covering the sand.

The youngster exclaimed disappointedly.

The water receded, etching little rivers of sand and

erasing the heel marks.

Ben emitted a quiet sigh of relief as the man laughed while bending over and peering at what remained after the sea's work. The child and parents dismissed the matter quickly from their minds, but only after a quick look around to satisfy the youngster's inquisitiveness. A while later, after having tossed some pebbles along the water and scattered some seagulls which had settled on a distant mossy rock, the trio withdrew and vanished in the direction from whence they came.

Sucking the salt air deep into his lungs, Ben checked about him and proceeded again on his journey, which continued now without further incident until his destination was reached.

The door to the farmhouse was locked, leaving little choice for Ben except to wait patiently in the small rundown barn. The livestock ignored him, although the chickens cackled uncomfortably for several seconds.

He sat back in the cover of some hay in a corner. Before him was a window which looked out from the rear of the barn onto the sloping hills to the Adriatic. His thoughts momentarily dwelled on the recent occurrences, and Coranis, whom he must wait for. Also, his mind went out to Talya Laylo and her security which gave him the deepest concern. Had it been right to let her return to the boat, possibly to be harmed? Ben could not be certain of her attitude now that she was aware of the death of Carlo. She did not know of the tumbling, death—stricken Bartholomew Free. Perhaps it would make no difference. There would be confusion. What she might piece together was sheer conjecture. It must have been the work of Coranis. Now, where was Coranis?

Ben had to restrain himself; his actions must be for only the purpose of his assignment. Nothing else. The assignment, the assignment sounded in his brain.

He drew the paper from his trouser pocket, holding it

gently, carefully. This was it. It happened so quickly. Free, Talya, the chasing of the unknown missile thrower, the death of Carlo, her tears, her anguish.

As he unraveled the paper, he saw the well-defined ink characters. It was obvious she had spent much time in its preparation. It was apparent that her thinking was methodical. She used great care in the writing of this paper; a piece of paper of such great importance to many people. Ben did not know the tremendous importance of her writings, but he suspected.

He read slowly Talya's words which were a copy from the intercepted message of Ambassador Joshua Pope. Here, in the strange environment of an old barn along the slopes of Albania, in the middle of a warm afternoon above the Adriatic, he read the meaning of Operation Baffle. The unmistakable voice of Ambassador Pope sounded in the words.

"The correct facts handed me within minutes of my departure from Vietnam as follows and I hope our informant can sooner deliver them through our office in Saigon."

The informant, the agent, Ben recalled, was dead. He had not traveled beyond Saigon.

"There is extensive damage planned by a secret revolutionary organization called Pi—Lpi."

Here Ben recalled certain information compiled by Jock Gumper on Bartholomew Free.

"The chief of the Pi-Lpi is Gregory Stavros."

"There are many agents in his command.

"Fissionable material in the most unique form and exact mechanism has entered the USA by importing in various methods, usually children's toys. The same has occurred carefully and systematically over a period of five years."

Free, the importer of toys, undoubtedly had been the means towards this end, the surreptitious smuggling in of fissionable material.

"The points selected for destruction are the missile sites

of Cape Kennedy; the research centers at Los Alamos; the physical research center in Houston; the aircraft development center in Los Angeles; and the industrial research center in Detroit."

Talya risked her life to hand this information to him. Did she realize its importance? If she did, it seemed she would have insisted the information be brought to light sooner. Perhaps she was not fully convinced. If the facts are too great for comprehension, they might appear false.

"The following men have been chosen.

"Arthur S. Brier, Cape Kennedy.

"Monroe V. Punfret, Los Alamos.

"Jay Piscomore, Houston.

"Walter Buswell, Los Angeles.

"Clayton Brozto, Detroit.

"They have been systematically drugged and, although appearing obviously normal, are triggered by various devices to perform certain functions by Stavros and his party.

"On the day chosen, precisely at three in the afternoon in the East, they will proceed to their assembled devices and insert the triggering portion. Once started, the resulting explosion cannot be stopped. It is estimated that each facility will be demolished and the damage will extend somewhat beyond a one-mile radius. All will be destroyed in the blast, leaving no witnesses.

"These men will be started on their course that morning by a commercial which shall appear at eight in the morning on a television news broadcast. The observance of this item will trigger their subconscious, hypnotic sleep."

The comprehension of the destruction plotted by Stavros was staggering. It seemed inconceivable that the mind of a man could be so fiendish. Ben no longer questioned whether the facts were real or unreal, whether the scheme was intended or unintended for fulfillment, whether the monstrous plan was within the realm of possibility or not. Now as he remained here amid this strange and almost unreal environment, aware of the impending, descending sword of doom, only one thought vibrated within his mind. He must be resolute. What he knew, must be passed along quickly and carefully as possible to prevent delay and error. He realized that, much as he planned, he must wait and hope for the early, safe return of Coranis!

What Talya had failed to learn in her copying of Ambassador Pope's letter? The intentions of Operation Baffle were there, the means, the points intended for desolation were described, and the tremendously important individual names were recited, the human keys (despite the fact their addresses had not been listed) to the prevention of the disasters.

The day, however, had not been mentioned.

How close were they to the hour of doom?

The sweat poured from Ben's forehead. Talya had said it would happen tomorrow, Thursday.

But today is Thursday! he remembered. In her mistreatment by Bartholomew Free she had confused the day.

Ben looked at his watch. When it was three on the East Coast of the United States, the havoc would occur.

It would require the information to be transmitted. An operator, he prayed, would be at his post on the opposite side of the Adriatic awaiting their message. But Coranis. Where was Coranis? Ben might be able to send a Mayday signal but that was all.

Ben remained in the barn, his impatience, fear, and whole being wrapped up in one ugly knot. His mouth was dry and he could not spit if he tried.

Alone, waiting, fearing they might fail, he had a moment for recollection. From his easy paced stay in the Sierras, life changed swiftly to a remote area above Tirana in Albania. Somehow, the two locales did not seem different. He still felt the solitude, thinking how swiftly the time passed when he received the call directing him to meet Ambassador

Pope. Life could change so quickly, sending him along a series of occurrences until his meeting with Regina.

What was it that seemed to possess her at times?

She had said on one occasion, "I doubt if anyone could remain continuously content, completely unaware of difficulties or worries. We must be thankful that we can forget– this is a blessing."

Perhaps something from the past was her discontent, the concerns of a past day. The something that grinds in all of us. Witness to life, how could one possibly avoid all the heartaches and pains that the passing days offered.

"Here we are, all part of this day, just as I am waiting. There is a quietness in this land and where I am, but it is merely a cover. Every day something is happening, and today no less than the others, but more for me," were Ben's thoughts.

It was not harmful to consider the past days. Ben could look back on the bad and the good. What the days had resolved themselves to was the defeat of Operation Baffle. It could not be achieved until the successful passing of the information over the waters of the Adriatic to whoever waited on the other side.

He decided that in the event Coranis did not appear in time, only one avenue was left to him. Ben would show himself to the Albanian authorities and plead his case. It was a chance. They would never believe him, he was certain, and would consider him mad. Or, if they finally were impressed, the tragic hour might already have passed. Was it possible to put a call through on a phone to Sergi in Rome? Again, "Who are you, an American? How did you come here? An agent of the imperialists." Still this was the only other hope. If Coranis did not show up shortly, he would have to make his move.

He thought of Regina; that would help him. And to think back how it had all happened. That first day waiting in San Francisco for Ambassador Pope's arrival. Step by step, the intrigue brought him to Washington and Regina.

The afternoon grew grayer; some clouds passed inland

from over the water. He recalled Talya. He must save her. If it rained again, they would be in trouble. Thankfully, he thought, they are stratus clouds and not the thick, black cumulonimbus. Perhaps, for this day, he may have some good fortune.

And where is Coranis?

Ben placed his cap on his head and stood up; he must not for an instant doze.

This was a fantastic plot. He recalled reading in the newspaper about hypnotic sleep induced on television. The idea had great possibilities for transgressions; the times would have to be directed to a period of restraint.

A winged creature flew up from the fields. Nothing else moved.

He prepared to leave, climb to the main road. Coranis had said a town lay close beyond.

His body trembled as he made to the door.

Then he heard it. The Coranis whistle, a crazy Greek tune.

His head showed first supporting a cap at a jaunty angle; then his shoulders; and his body, as he made his way.

"You crazy bugger, Coranis," Ben said aloud. "Can't you hurry?"

They leaned back now. They were on their cots. They prayed the message had been properly received on the Italian side.

It was a hectic time. At first, they thought to code and actually started to do so.

Coranis said: "This is no good. We will lose too much time."

He was almost saying, let's forget it, they'll catch on to this place shortly, anyway; it was good while it lasted, we might as well go for broke. He would give a kiss of death to a home he had known for the last two years.

So, the message was sent straight for anyone to know and read if they wished. Word came back that the Italian side had received, and now Ben and Coranis lay back on their cots, mopping the sweat from their faces.

"I can almost die now," Ben exploded. He had fulfilled his mission with the help of so many. He hoped Ambassador Pope's death had not been in vain. Time would tell.

Now there were Sebastian Giorgio and Talya Laylo to save if they could.

Coranis told his story.

"When I threw the stones, this man you call Free followed me. He can run fast," Coranis said, rubbing his beard with the back of his hand, "but not fast enough to catch me. I am getting older, but my legs are still good." He laughed as though he recalled something humorous. "He carried a gun and he was ready to use it on me, I knew, if he could find me.

"Ben, that man had the face of the devil, and it is good he is dead."

Ben swallowed a glass of brandy in one continuous drink. He knew he could finish the bottle without feeling it. He felt exhilarated. He succeeded. If need be, he knew, he could face death without flinching.

"It is hard to say a man deserves to die," Ben said, "but Bartholomew Free was the most foul person I have ever known."

"I had my knife ready, in case," Coranis continued.

Ben figured that this was what had done the job.

"Then he moved away and some distance from me. I saw this other man, this fat man. Free did not see him. Apparently, he followed Free. How long he was watching, I do not know. It was as if he came from nowhere."

This discussion followed the transmission of their message. For the first time, Ben was learning why Coranis was delayed.

"He circled around to get behind this Free, you could see. For a while, I thought to myself, Ben, Free might think this fat man threw the stones. And maybe he thought so. When he started back, the fat man came out of the bushes behind him and said something to the other."

The expressive Coranis acted the part. "Like this, the little man does; his hands in the air, and he turns around to face the fat man.

"Free could not have said five words. There was a flash from the fat man's gun, no noise, and Free fell down."

Refreshing his face with some cool water, Ben interrupted his toweling. "Coranis, I thought it was you."

"No, Ben, it was not me. That's why I could not get back. It was well you returned. Together, we may never have managed, or you would have walked into a trap."

Coranis took a longer drink than Ben's and continued to speak as if he had imbibed water. To Ben, Coranis' face was the happiest sight in the world.

"The fat man signaled for some others to come up from the distance and they searched and searched. I waited a long time to be sure. I could not take a chance who they were. I did not know who they were."

"But we saw Free. How was it possible?" Ben asked.

"Ah, yes, the little man felt it, but he was not dead yet. He was like a drunken man. You saw him then, in his last walk of death. Before I returned here, I checked, and they carried his body away."

Thus ended Coranis' tale. He was fortunate to elude the others. It could only be assumed that they were part of Stavros' party.

If this were so, then the fact was indisputable. Talya and Sebastian Giorgio were in grave danger. The fat man, there was a good suspicion, may have seen Coranis.

It was a foregone conclusion Ben and Coranis needed

to act fast. With the good fortune they prayed for, they might succeed.

Ben pledged his life, if necessary, to his endeavor. Coranis, who had faced death many times, did not debate the question or give it any consideration.

The last message was sent by Coranis and this was coded. It advised that he must abandon his position.

And the time for their pickup was established to be two a.m. at the rendezvous where Ben previously had been put ashore.

The time that Ben and Talya had agreed upon was all-important now. It seemed an unfortunate time to have selected, for it permitted Stavros and the others the opportunity to learn whether their work of five years had succeeded.

It seemed inconceivable that, as they lie in darkness, the evil machinations of one man could be affecting the lives of many, thousands of miles away and bathed in the light of day.

Coranis said, transferring a kiss from his hands to the transmitting equipment, "Farewell, you have treated me well."

He placed a charge and detonator set to explode at three in the morning at the rear of the equipment.

"There will be nothing left of this," and he showed his concern, "but the animals will be safe. I hate to leave them behind."

When they started on their way, Coranis locked the door and patted the side of the farmhouse fondly. "Ah, well, it could not have lasted forever. Not even the Parthenon." His joke was, "In a million years, it will mean nothing. Then that is such a long time, I cannot imagine it."

As they walked down to where the boat was concealed, the atmosphere seemed to Ben the same as the time of his arrival; the calm night, the feeling of softness in the air. Coranis carried two plastic charges and detonators which he was fond of using. It was a few years back when he last used such implements. This night he thought would be filled with the sounds of violent explosions. This was an exaggeration, but it gave him an opportunity to recall his youth and the carefree hours when the earth's concerns seemed not to be his problems.

For the boat Ben carried a small motor that Coranis had tied to Ben's back. So, all in all, they were both well employed, a fact that distracted their attention away from any anxieties they might have.

Ben hoped that Operation Baffle had been foiled. This he would not know until the hour passed. When he considered the nearness of the time, he became aware of a cold sweat on his forehead.

Besides his arsenal for defense, Coranis also carried along the transistor radio. With this, they could obtain reports of the news and world developments. They were surely interested in the great cause they had served.

Fourteen

THE BOAT LAY PEACEFULLY where they had secured it. They moved it into the cool water and paddled slowly away from shore. The motor was set in place, but was not used until they were well away from land.

Ben gazed at his watch which indicated eight-thirty. They had exactly one hour to traverse the few miles, set a position some distance from the yacht, and meet with Talya who would swim out to them.

If their plans were successful, they would set a direction north and then head in for shore. Talya would be left behind while they made an attempt to penetrate the yacht and set Sebastian Giorgio free. Talya would be given instructions to proceed along the coast to the inlet where she was to wait for their return. She would be given a flashlight to signal in the event Ben and Coranis failed to find her.

This was a difficult task they were undertaking. After the serious episode they had just experienced, they could face any eventuality.

They moved along the coast at a moderate speed. They passed the region where Talya walked to that afternoon. It was suggested by Coranis that this might be the spot they would leave Talya. From this point to the inlet, as Ben found earlier, the walking was fairly easy and free of obstructions.

Finally they could see the lights of the yacht and the homes of Sarka, the small resort area. Coranis headed out to sea and made a series of ninety degree turns before he cut the motor and they drifted in the ocean's currents. Now began the task of paddling slowly towards the direction of the yacht. It loomed larger and more distinct. Some figures could be seen on the deck. It appeared as a quiet, ominous scene.

Ben pointed to a dimly outlined object. "That must be the raft, Coranis. See there, the one Talya mentioned."

Coranis shook his head. "I will go a little closer, but we have to be careful. The tide is moving in and we do not want to be carried too close."

"Talya will have the tide to swim against," Ben said.

Coranis replied: "It is not bad. She will have no trouble."

They sat quietly now and waited.

Coranis' thoughts went back to the last war. As a young man in his twenties, he had traveled from his native Greece to Albania to repel the fascists. It was guerrilla war. The arms to defend themselves were few. The knowledge of the terrain, the surprise assault, and the quick withdrawal were their only real means of defense. It was nothing new to fight this way, but it did not guarantee success. They lost many, and the invaders lost many. It was the hell of war for people who wanted to live peacefully. Could he imagine how a farmer living in the hills he was born to and satisfied with the moderate means available to him was interested in the politics of war? They never wanted these problems, Coranis thought, but, perhaps, they should have taken an interest before as they were required to do afterwards.

He had lost his wife and only child during those terrible days. He would not think of it again.

Maybe, he felt, he saw something of himself in this young man, Ben Ford, who sat quietly across from him. Did he not mention the day before to Coranis how he had a deep love for a young woman and must not fail to return to her? This was the love that he, Coranis, once knew. He thought well of Ben; it was an obligation for Coranis to see that Ben would return to the woman he spoke about joyfully.

A few minutes passed the agreed upon hour. There was the meeting scheduled with the Albatross of Pesce at two a.m. They knew now they had played it too closely. Pesce would wait, Coranis said, but he would not wait too long for fear of the patrols that might be out. The patrols were fighting the continuous smuggling that went on in these waters. Pesce knew much of their habits, but the longer one lingered, the greater became the danger.

Ben said: "I can't leave her this way, Coranis. If only because of what she has done to help us. I must find out what is going on."

Coranis would not prevent Ben in his decision, nor did he try very hard.

Ben removed his outer clothing, eased himself over the side of the boat, and slid almost noiselessly into the cool water. He swam away from Coranis who intently watched and muttered, "Good luck," absently to himself.

Ben's course carried him slightly away from the raft and towards the stern of the yacht. He swam with a strength and a determination he had never realized before and with the greatest care; if observed, it would be over. The thought of Talya was in his mind.

He waded along the side of the yacht, spying a ship's ladder a few feet away. What could he do now but hope to learn something of what had occurred to delay Talya. He could not storm the boat and overcome the crew. Perhaps she was no longer aboard; he did not know. He certainly held no knowledge of what transpired from the time she disappeared along the beach on her way back to the yacht. And, at the time of her leaving, neither one of them knew Free had been shot.

The several seconds felt like hours as he waited, trying to decide if he should climb the white painted ladder beyond.

Above him, voices came playfully.

"Okay, Talya, show them what you can do. A swan dive, Talya."

"Beautiful, Talya," another voice shouted.

Talya's sleek form splashed the water near Ben and she vanished in the cold depths. When she surfaced, she shook the water from her eyes and searched for the direction of the raft.

She played her part well, Ben thought. She succeeded.

Above, the voices continued.

"A marvelous body," one said.

"It seems a pity," another said.

"Wait until she has swum a few feet away," the harsh voice of the first one spoke. "Then, flash the beam. You can pick up the whiteness of the bikini on her back. Then, step away. It will only take one shot."

Ben's hand tightened on the line he managed to grab hold of. Talya did not see him; she began to swim away in strong, even strokes. He realized the villains intended to shoot her. What could he do? He must act quickly. He prayed for time as he grasped the ship's ladder.

"Show us how fast you can swim," the venom of the second man came.

Looking back over his shoulder as he crouched along the bottom tread of the ladder, Ben could see Talya was approaching midway to the raft.

"We cannot let her get too far away, Manfred," the voice of the second man spoke again.

Ben was at the top step and could peer along the expanse of the deck. The surroundings were ornate and expensive. The oaken deck was clean and orderly. Ben was puzzled by the obvious activity. The crew was making haste to leave.

At the stern where they stood above him, Ben saw Manfred, sighting along the length of an automatic carbine while another man readied the spotlight.

"Talya shall be the only remembrance of our days in Albania," Manfred spoke out as the other laughed.

Suddenly, there was a shaking of the craft. The twin-screw began to turn from the force of the ship's engine. There was a noticeable swaying movement.

Talya stopped momentarily to turn and watch.

Manfred sighted more carefully.

It was now for Ben, as the hand of the second man moved towards the switch which would send a beam of light flashing upon the image of Talya in the Adriatic. It was the great effort, the summoning of all strength, the crashing of the mind, heart, body and soul in one grand action, the overwhelming surge to destroy.

Ben rushed from his position with one thought; to catch the duo with one body-breaking charge, toppling them over the stern, if possible.

He may have been a second too late as the light flashed along the blackened night. Ben thought he heard a shot, but the swift action was beyond reflection. He caught Manfred by surprise and sent him reeling; Manfred spun backwards into the brine. Ben recovered from the shock of impact as the second man rose from his prone position to attack him. He lunged, but Ben caught him about the waist, carrying his adversary with him over the ship's side and into the splash of the water. Ben lost hold of him as they swirled into the depths. But now, as Ben surfaced and caught the air again in his lungs, he saw the struggling second man before him being sucked toward the screws of the yacht. There was a gnashing and grinding as the boat slowly moved out. Ben shut his eyes and swam away.

In this fleeting instant, he forgot Manfred, an error he could not allow himself as steely, thin fingers caught him about the throat from behind. His senses swirled and he felt himself swallowing salt water and sinking below the ocean's surface. Tiredness struck him. He felt he was at death's door.

Then the hands released themselves, and were no longer dangerous. Manfred floated unevenly upon the water, dead, his head against the hull of a boat, Coranis' boat. Ben felt Coranis' hands lifting him from the water and placing him in the bottom of the boat. The purr of the boat's motor was lost in the sound from the yacht aside it.

The beam of the searchlight was no more; a well-placed shot from Coranis' gun spelled its doom.

Ben lay exhausted with the salt of the ocean in his mouth and lungs. He could feel the spurt of power that Coranis fed into the motor as they spun away from the yacht. And he heard the clamor of voices from the ship's gunwale.

Coranis headed for the raft where Talya Laylo sat bleeding from a wound in her arm. The blood made a crimson smear on her white bikini.

This was the astonishment, that they were not pursued. They waited now as the vessel moved further away from them into the open sea.

"They are anxious to leave," said Coranis. "They must fear something." He turned on the transistor while they waited. The heated voice of a Greek announcer spoke lengthily, with occasional breaks from other voices.

"What is it?" Ben asked.

Coranis grinned. "Nothing important. Results of the soccer matches."

"They kept me locked up when I returned," spoke Talya, weakly. Her face was pallid under the stars. With great tenderness, Coranis placed her in the boat and momentarily stopped the bleeding with a tourniquet from his shirt. To prevent her trembling, Coranis removed his shirt and trousers and covered her body.

It seemed ludicrous to Ben to see Coranis at the tiller

with only his old woolen underwear.

The yacht was now well away from land.

Talya said, "They did not say anything to me. But, when I insisted I must swim, they laughed. It seemed I did not understand."

Ben had recovered his strength again. "Don't trouble yourself," he said. "it is over."

With one final inspection about him, Coranis began the passage to their meeting with Pesce.

It was after they had started and proceeded a safe distance from the yacht that they heard an earsplitting explosion. The yacht was torn asunder with an immense blast, and fire enveloped completely that which remained upon the water. The light of the blazing hull illuminated the sky, the ocean and the town of Sarka. Ben could see the fire's brightness on the faces of Talya and Coranis. All could feel the traveling concussion in the water and the wash of the waves that followed. The remnants of the yacht sank quickly, but while the light remained, Ben caught what seemed the image of a fat man climbing the main road of Sarka and shaking his fist in defiance to the sky.

Gregory Stavros often stated there would be few witnesses remaining alive on that fateful day.

Fifteen

WALTER BUSWELL AWAKENED early that Thursday morning as was his habit on every morning of the work week. When his eyes caught the rays of the first sunlight, he noticed a slight anxiety that remained in his mind from the evening before. It was strange how brilliant the light could be and how cheerful the chirping of the birds could sound, and yet, there was in Walter's feelings a sort of resentment to that moment and the day.

He was utterly dissatisfied, he could object to the sparrow perched in the nearby apple tree which he spied below the half drawn shade. Since there was nothing particular to gain from conversation with bird life, he refrained from saying anything and thought rather of the work outlined for his completion on this date. For some reason not evident to himself, the idea struck him that he had some work to attend to around noontime. Exactly what it was, he had forgotten. He must remember to look on his note pad at the office.

What welled up within him now was the thought he would like to have slept longer, wishing it were Saturday or Sunday, but he must arise, nevertheless, and travel to a day's task for which he found no desire.

He sat up in his bed and ran his hands through his sandy hair, then along the stubble of one day's growth of beard. He proceeded at a moderate pace and fashion to shower and prepare himself for the pleasantries and aggravations of the day.

While he mused, and worked pulling on his socks, the recollection struck him that he must watch the television news broadcast at eight a.m. Switching on the set, he gained some satisfaction in the fact that lately he was more prone to remain in touch with public affairs, both national and international. Certainly the times offered much to learn because of the recent growth of the news media. The last ten years alone showed an unparalleled change in the transmission of facts throughout the world.

"Aha!" he exclaimed as the picture brightened on the tube and he stepped closer to the set to focus the image. It was yet early for the broadcast, a full hour to go. His exclamation came because lately the set behaved erratically, taking some time to warm up, but he had grown attached to it and preferred it to the sleek new gold and brown portable that his dear friend entrusted him with before his recent departure.

"Be so kind, Walter," Stavros said, "to take good care of my set until my next visit. I see your television is still operating efficiently, but you may please use mine if you have any difficulty with your own."

Walter did not understand the completeness of Stavros' preparations for all eventualities in the carrying out of his scheme. Simply, what seemed Stavros' continuous, kind considerations had no other basis for Walter than the fact he was a generous, kind gentleman. Walter did not suspect the other's schemes.

The station at this moment was projecting the sounds and visage of a composer of modern sophisticated lyrics which portrayed the American urban scene. It was somewhat foreign to Walter's ear since he was still used to the simple-lined ballads of the Thirties and Forties. He held little interest in modern compositions–even as they applied to the more classical style. Mainly his appreciation went along the lines of Gershwin and Rodgers in the twentieth century vein, and Beethoven and Chopin and Bach, and some of the Italian operas in the classical music.

He hummed along in a melodic line as the station changed at the hour, and the broadcaster in a deep resonant voice announced the news. The news began with the latest information on Vietnam, some rumblings around Singapore, with a swift jump to Greece. This Walter liked. The strange names came thick and fast.

Was it possible that, in the past, there were so many hot spots in the world? He imagined so. Now it was more pronounced because of the swift transmission of the daily news. This caused him to smile; many difficulties existed in all periods of the historical world, and easily the escapades of Napoleon or Hannibal could have been broadcast if broadcasting existed. Walter's mind could not seriously conceive a news report of an attack of prehistoric animals and the wanderings of the ancient man. It was ludicrous that the books always pictured this hapless individual hunched over, with thick hair, a grotesque face, and with the ever present, loosely hanging club.

Walter watched the news broadcast with an intensity unusual for him. When the local news began, a few new stories were reported by the announcer, and then, abruptly, a commercial interrupted. This abruptness was really commonplace since it was difficult always to announce, "This is a commercial."

Buswell found a particular interest in this advertisement which recited the opportunity that existed now in certain research work. Of course, this was the one he was recently attracted to that led to his association with Stavros. The repetition of it held no particular interest to him now, despite the fact he had not seen it for some time. What caught his attention was the manner in which a certain sign was portrayed on a door to opportunity and the television camera zeroed into the knob of the door, an obvious brass knob with the tiny delicate edging of tracery and the gentle floating figure. Walter's eyes fixed determinedly upon this image, but he was unaware of the sudden change in his attitude that occurred at that precise moment.

A part of his brain could have asked, Does he carry that damned knob with him everywhere? But it had no chance of overcoming the reasoning that swept through Walter's thoughts. What he could not recall he had to do at noontime and for which he was going to consult his note pad, now came resolutely forward.

"Yep, yep," he spoke so that anyone present might have heard. "The trial run on this brilliant experiment. This is very important to all of us."

Now he remembered well to the finest details, exactly how he must conduct himself, where to proceed, when to proceed, the exact time for the insertion of the sparking mechanism.

The drive to the office was a pleasant one for him along the shore drive, watching the early bathers, surfers and boaters who were out early enjoying the warmth of the comfortable day. He remembered to drive carefully with an unusual precaution. This was not unlike him, to drive carefully. Yet, this day he was proceeding with the utmost confidence that anything he might undertake he would be successful.

The air that swept along the shoreline struck him soothingly. It called for a dip in the ocean later in the day after he completed his work. Maybe he could break away early. The following day was Friday, and was left for summing up.

Nobody really was wont to break his arse, as Wilbur Foxbit stated in his decidedly New England accent. Walter had no particular other idea but to swim since he was an excellent swimmer and saw no necessity in chasing the girls as the beach boys could be seen doing. Every once in a while, a group of nature boys with their bulging biceps and overdeveloped physiques would carry on their games along the sand. Certainly there was much to be seen and enjoyed at the seaside.

The guard let him drive past the gate. "Hi there, Freddie. It looks maybe it will be a pleasant warm day today," Walter greeted him.

Freddie responded with, "Hello, Mr. Buswell. You appear chipper this morning. Anything big going today?"

Walter laughed back. "If there is, I'll let you know about it." Humorously he considered how this guard whom he had known well for several years must depend on his own keenness and his continuous vigilance in these perilous times.

The morning passed slowly for Walter. Somehow he was snowed under with an accumulation of paperwork and, if he had no reason to return to his office from the laboratory that morning, he would have found it in the necessity of returning to reduce the pile.

Unbeknownst to Walter Buswell was the fact that Coranis' message, once received by the operator on the opposite side of the Adriatic, sped swiftly along the channels of communication across the Atlantic and to the desk of Mark Crescent.

Clarissa Neale, in all excitement, crashed in on Crescent's conference as she was instructed to do in the event of any word from overseas.

The suddenly perturbed Crescent, jolted from his concentration, turned abruptly towards Clarissa, and was about to explode in a volley of curses when he caught his tongue and control and said: "What is it now, Miss Neale?"

"John Sergi," she replied hesitantly, "from Rome."

"All right, all right, what the hell does he want now?" His abrupt question came to the slight dismay of the two men with him.

Clarissa Neale who, until then, was the picture of restraint in her relationship to her boss finally succumbed to the pressure of her position.

"Dammit, Mr. Crescent, get on the phone before someone blows us to hell! Sergi says so!"

Crescent was overwhelmed. He withheld the who the hell is Sergi to say so, and diplomatically he relieved the momentary tenseness with, "Bless you, Miss Neale, you may damned well be right. I'm sorry. Excuse me, gentlemen. We can talk about this later."

The two men folded up their documents and departed, wishing they each had a secretary as delightfully attractive as Clarissa Neale.

Crescent listened intently on the phone for a brief introduction to what Sergi was reporting. When it was apparent that what he had to say was the hottest thing on earth, and that the speed of light was necessary to prevent disaster, a bead of sweat swept over Crescent's forehead and the phone seemed about to crack under his grip.

"Get on this, Miss Neale," he shouted across the room through the open door which Clarissa had left ajar.

She worked rapidly writing the information from Ambassador Pope with special attention to the names, while the phone was also tied in immediately to a recording device.

Together they worked feverishly to key in all the necessary departments and offices.

Dr. Flair quickly crossed over from his office when he got the news what had developed.

His lean face perused the copy over Crescent's shoulder as the latter worked nonstop.

Finally, Mark spoke with Kyle Sanders in San Francisco after the Los Angeles office and Federal office were tied in on the name, Walter Buswell.

Kyle said: "I'm on it, Mark. Faster than hell."

That Thursday morning, Buswell left the research laboratory at exactly eleven forty-five a.m. and headed in a somewhat rigid walk towards his office. Unexpectedly for Buswell but still prepared for the occurrence, Freddie the guard was walking the long narrow corridor towards his locker room since he had been relieved at his post, and he bumped into Walter.

"Hi, there, Mr. Buswell, what'cher up to?" he picked up the banter of the early morning.

"Nothing, nothing," Walter stammered, and the embarrassment showed in his face. "Why do you ask?"

"Like you said you'd let me know if something was going to happen."

Freddie noticed the strangeness in Buswell's visage, the glassy stare in his eyes. He never figured Buswell to be influenced by the bottle. This was his only suspicion. What a heck of a nice guy to be hitting the bottle. Must be something bothering him. Too many parties, probably. He's single. Why not. It gets them after a while.

"That's right, Freddie, that's right," Walter responded, and he recited stiffly, "You will excuse me, Freddie. I have an extremely important call to make home. You will excuse me."

"Of course," Freddie replied as the pressure on his arm by Buswell to pass suggested some serious annoyance or far more troublesome difficulty.

Freddie stood scratching his head as he watched the unsteady gait of Buswell along the corridor. "Why in the heck would he be calling home? He isn't married," he muttered to himself. This seemed reasonable since married men had all the troubles, according to Freddie the guard.

Buswell looked at his watch as he sat down in his office, momentarily overcome by an oppressive heat. It was nine minutes before the hour.

I simply cannot understand what this is all about, he wanted to say and believe, but the uncontrollable suggestive force compelled him to continue. He was not fearful or hesitant. Still there was a suspicion something was not right. The essential ability he lost was to analyze. He was performing mechanically and, despite the fact he did not especially desire to do so, he continued to behave in a parading soldier fashion. He was the toy and the spring had been wound some time ago.

At exactly five minutes before the hour, he would begin to assemble the triggering mechanism. He took his key and opened the locked drawer of the desk and set the few parts before him. Then he watched carefully as the seconds continued to tick and the time for assembling would occur. The seconds seemed longer, but they were still seconds. His disturbed state made him wonder what it meant by their slow ticking. A whole lifetime collected now before him as he watched the gradual nearing to the five minutes before the hour. The second hand of the carefully timed watch passed the twelve and continued by. It was now that time.

Walter assembled the parts with stiff, bent fingers. They went together with difficulty, so it seemed. Stavros had not expected this or prepared for it. Perhaps he had not allowed sufficient time, but really, what did it matter whether the detonation went off at the precise minute or slightly after. He wanted to coordinate as closely as possible, thus avoiding mishap.

Buswell now had the pieces together; the ineptness passed. All that was needed now was the triggering part. It was three minutes to the simulated detonation.

What had he said? When should the device be inserted?

Buswell ran his fingers uncontrollably along his face.

The shiny, silvery device before him lay vengefully upon the desk. He suspected that the eyes that stared from the silvery piece were the eyes of the devil, and that the silent device was speaking a gibberish, a language unknown to him, a language of the devil and his hell.

For what reason he did not know but the impulse was there; Walter Buswell picked up the shiny metal and flung it in a paroxysm of hatred through the opaque glass light of the door.

The glass splintered and crashed to the floor. The metal piece pounded vibrantly as it ricocheted along the corridor and came to rest at the feet of Freddie, who was returning to check on the condition of his friend. Within seconds, there were many faces at the door.

Kyle Sanders, meanwhile, had stepped from the shadows of a cabinet in Walter's office.

"Thank God, it's over," Kyle said, as he held Walter's arm. "C'mon, Mr. Buswell, you'll be okay now."

Buswell did not resist. But he looked down into the empty lower drawer of the file as Sanders held it open.

Sixteen

THE LAST TRACE OF night had disappeared on the arrival of Pesce's boat in Brindisi. Sergi, offering congratulations, personally had come to meet Ben.

"You beat them, Ben," he said. "It was close. There was a chance it might have come off. It was a mechanically sound device. And then these men they had made tools of. It is an unanswered question whether they all would have performed against their will. It's early yet to say much, but they will be taken care of. The important thing is your success, and your safety."

It was in that order, too, Ben knew. The success of the mission was the most important. It would be that way in the future. There was no questioning laying down your life for your friend. If there had been before, that question did not exist now. Patriotism was somewhat different now. It was a necessity, and a fight against the forces of evil.

Talya Laylo developed a fever and, for a few moments on their return upon the Albatross, appeared terribly sick. An ambulance carried her off to a hospital in Brindisi where Ben visited her later that same day.

"I have only you to thank and that kind Coranis. He is a wonderful man. It seems sad that he cannot be more happy."

"He is," Ben assured, "as long as he has his brandy and a little jig to do."

"I know, Ben, but without a good woman as he has known, it must be difficult for him."

"You have seen a lot, poor Talya," Ben spoke. "What shall you do now?"

"I will manage," she replied, "as always. I have lost one whom I loved. I shall lose another now."

Talya felt it was unfair to speak to Ben this way.

"You must have many women friends in your life, Ben. Is it true?"

He placed his finger against her lips.

"You talk too much, Talya."

"But men are the same with desires," she pursued. "But you are different. Women must be attracted to you. Maybe it is your kindness and attention, and sometimes in little ways. Coming here to see me when you must have many important matters elsewhere." She hesitated and coyly asked, "What is she like, Ben?"

"Who?"

"This girl you love?"

"Well, now, that is hard to say. She is like the first budding of the rose in the early summer, her cheeks their soft pastel red; her eyes are cool and placid as the surface of a mountain lake, her nose was stolen from a cherub, and her lips are the softness of a thousand clouds in a lazy, sleepy hamlet. That just comes off the top of my head."

"It must be wonderful that you love her this way." She crumpled her silken handkerchief. "I must stop, Ben, I am being unkind."

"Yes, you are," he said, and motioned to leave. "I do

have to get back to Rome and file my report."

She held his hand.

"You will remember me sometimes, Ben?"

"I shall never forget you."

He kissed her on the lips and recalled that, "This is a woman, my gosh, this is a wonderful woman."

Before they departed the coast of Albania that early morning, things did not proceed as Ben expected.

Coranis managed to reach the inlet. They waited a while for Pesce to arrive; some anxiety was spent in the thought that he might not show.

As Pesce explained: "When I see that explosion and light, I thought the world had come to an end. But I did not give up. I figured they may need me more. It is maybe more dangerous now with the patrol boats, but, then again, maybe they will all head to Sarka."

This assumption proved correct in that Ben and the others later saw the patrol boats heading southward towards the explosion. For a time it seemed that it would be their undoing. Coranis, however, held closely to the shore and was forced to beach on one occasion to avoid interception. This all lent to the finish of a most trying episode.

"Anyway," Pesce continued, "I am successful in avoiding them and that is the important thing."

Coranis, however, hesitated when time came for their departure from the inlet, not, as he explained, that he was concerned about the trip to Brindisi, which no one wanted or expected him to say, his valor being a monument to Greek resistance, but because, as he said, "Aw, hell, you go. I stay here. They will not find me. I will be all right and back in business again."

The explosion of the yacht changed Coranis' mind, for he reasoned that those who might suspect him and lead to his apprehension were now dead. He had visions of a watch over the farmhouse and by careful observation, determining whether it was still safe.

Ben said: "We can't make you come. It is up to you to convince yourself you shall be safe."

"I will be, do not worry."

"We shall miss you, good old Coranis, we shall miss you immensely."

"Some day, maybe you will visit me, if it is possible."

Ben could not now that easily forget his debt to this man. He embraced him warmly without embarrassment.

"So that you can save my life again."

"Not so," Coranis said. "So I can play cards with you and we have a drink." Coranis wanted to say, "and you can bring your new wife to see me," but it brought back memories of his own saddened life.

Thus they had left him on the sandy shore of the inlet. Coranis' last words that Ben would always remember were, "Hell, I almost forgot. I got to get to my house before she explodes." He spoke as he ran upwards from the cove. And he was successful, thank God, Ben thought for they failed to see or hear any later explosion.

Here in Rome he would do what the Romans do. Instructions he gave to Sergi were that he was not to be disturbed. He wanted to rest; and he would make his report shortly. Sergi agreed.

The news on the successful destruction of Operation Baffle was partially released. Ben wanted no part of the hand shaking and congratulations. That sort of thing wearied him.

He wondered what he would be called. Perhaps it would be difficult to understand that he was employed and paid by the Diplomatic Corp to troubleshoot on problems and coordinate for the peace and well-being of all. If he succeeded in his work, he was satisfied. It was as simple as that; his position was not unique except that he may have put more work into it.

In Rome, he ran to Regina Terchenka.

"I told you, Regina, I would come back," he said on their first meeting together again at her hotel.

"Oh, God," she cried. "Ben, how I love you. How I feared that something might happen. The newspapers. I want to hear nothing. Except that you are safe and that you love me."

They spent that evening in the dining room below. It was a quaint room in a style that reminded of some long ago period in Italian history.

"I, a boy from Ohio, with the royalty of Hungary." He toasted, his glass raised on high, but she hesitated. "Why, what is the matter?" he asked.

"Because it is not true," she replied. "Perhaps there is some royal blood in me, but those times have passed, Ben. You must understand."

"Why do you say that?"

"I work for a Communist government, Ben; do you not take that into consideration?"

He would not be diverted. "You shall remain royalty. Anyway, there is a thaw in the cold war." He stroked the side of her face and countered, "Do you not realize that?"

"And what happened just a short while ago that you know so much about?"

"We certainly cannot blame the Hungarians, not that I should hold it against you."

She knew it was sad that they spoke this way. "Can you not see, Ben, if you do or don't blame the Hungarians, it makes no difference. You shall blame another Communist country and we are the Communists, we are the Communist Bloc." Her eyes shone their excitement. Ben had known her before this way.

"I shall not toast then," he relented, "if it pleases you."

"A toast, Ben, yes, to your success and our love."

They drank, and it seemed finished.

"Not to my success, Regina, because that might not be yours."

"Ben, I love you. Can you understand that only?"

"Yes. I will try to remember that and only that. What has happened yesterday, today, or shall happen at any time shall not concern me when it is you that I think of."

"So be it," she replied. "Ben, you are invincible."

Afterwards, they walked in the night of Rome.

Very little information on what had occurred off Sarka appeared in the newspapers. They seemed to be selling at a normal rate, as before.

"See Ben? The people do not comprehend what it is all about."

"You do comprehend, Regina?" he asked.

"What I know of it, it was a monstrous thing. But it seems something just as awful could happen again and again."

"And the answer is eternal vigilance.

"For an eternity of time?" she asked.

"What other way, then, Regina, what other way?"

Their love seemed remote by these conversations.

"Disarmament," he suggested.

"That would help," she said.

"What else is there?" he asked.

"Love, Ben, love. Love me always, always, always." And she fell into his arms with the fear and the fright upon her, and cold uncontrollable sweat covering her arms and face.

"What is it, Regina, that torments you So? Why do you seem to go on with this strange thought you have in you? I have seen it before."

"I know, I know," she replied. "Forgive me, Ben. Perhaps it was the fear of what might happen to you."

"But you knew nothing. Why should you fear? Tell me, perhaps I can help you."

They passed into a park where others were strolling, enjoying the evening's comfort far from the hot brightness of the day. After a while, they sat.

Ben felt fatigued. It had been an awful long day. And now Regina was troubled. He had looked forward to more of what was the day at Como.

"When I was a little girl, Ben, I did see something of the days you speak of. But I was little, and I remember so little now. It was the most difficult time. I shall never forget the war. It still seems to be so near to me now. I was perpetually frightened, and to be perpetually frightened as a child is an awful thing. We may grow up to be terrible creatures, but it seems that each succeeding generation owes something to the children to come."

Ben held her close and the anxiety seemed to have left her.

"We shall have lovely children, Regina, and we shall love them very much."

"If that could be," she said.

Not wanting to dispute against her feelings, Ben let this point pass. To him, everything could be and to think differently would not be his nature.

Seventeen

THE APPEARANCE OF GUMPER the following day cheered Ben. Jock Gumper hated to be a shut-in. To pass the days to his recovery he followed Ben's escapade as closely as he was permitted. Then, when the story broke, he received permission to journey over to Rome and meet his friend. After all, he had been some party to the goings on. And did he not get winged by one of Bartholomew Free's bullets?

Gumper said: "It's a real crazy one. This idea of tying the whole rotten caboodle in with television. It will give television a bad name."

Then he pulled out one of his cigars.

"It's been a long way, Ben. How do you feel?"

"Okay," Ben replied.

"You seem a little tired. Why don't you kick it and go up to one of these salt springs, Monte Zatini. It's not too far."

"Me in mud baths. You crazy, Gump?"

Gumper lit up and blew the smoke out.

"The girl, I bet."

Ben admitted: "Gumper, good old buddy, maybe you're right. I can tell you, maybe. Love's no easy matter."

"What's the matter, you think I don't know anything about it? A big fat guy like me. I got some charms. They don't all go for you curly-headed fellows."

Gumper emitted a laugh that shook the confines of Ben's room and the corridor beyond.

"It's just that she's on a different side of the iron curtain. Poses problems."

"I know," Gumper assured. "But you're in the Diplomatic Corp."

"Worse still."

"I'm sorry, Ben, I can't help you. But you'll work something out."

Their last thoughts at that meeting were on Kyle Sanders and Mark Crescent. Crescent had probably cursed harshly when they had broken Operation Baffle with Clarissa running to hide herself. Gumper said Crescent was satisfied how things worked out, and that no damage occurred.

Then they parted, with Gumper saying, "Crescent wants me to stick close to you until you get back. Then, it's back to the Frisco beat for me–where it all began."

There was nothing to think about for the next several days but Regina and how they could reconcile their lives. They spoke of a marriage that seemed remote because of her hesitancy. He could never forget, he never would. At least, she seemed calmed. Ben attributed her apparent anxiety as being caused by the terrible tempo of the past days.

His report was made and sent in to Sergi. Faithful to his promise, Sergi kept Ben out of the limelight and secured additional time for his stay over in Rome.

Ben secured the chalet at Como again, and he and Regina coursed the way in what, again, seemed unbelievably happy days.

Even a solution had been found to their marriage. She

would complete her work in two months and ask to be relieved of her duties. Through some influential individuals she knew, she would ask to be allowed to go to the States to marry Ben. It seemed it might take a long time but they could wait where it was necessary.

They laughed their way along the length of Como so that the citizens thought them unusual, even referring to Regina as the crazy American. This got to be quite a joke and Regina wore the name well.

Finally, it came the morning for their return trip to Rome. Ben good-naturedly chided her on the ride back at the spot where she stopped the car and fled into the field. She said she wanted to stop again, and he did. This time, there was no running, and no pursuit.

She merely wanted to say, "I shall cherish this moment forever, Ben. The sight of the people working in the fields, the soft quietness of the day, I can remember these things always. I thank you for letting me come here again." This love of the country came spontaneously.

"If anything should ever happen to us, you shall remember this place, Ben, where we stopped." She spoke oddly as she did at times before when Ben could not fathom the full meaning of her words.

He said: "I shall remember you. Here, on a quiet day, it happened."

"Do I make you sad, Ben?" she asked.

"Sometimes, as in moments like this when I am not sure I understand you."

"You need not try, Ben. It is feeling, the feeling of love that is important. And we have it here. It must be some association that I make of these surroundings with perfection. Here is the perfect world, the perfect day if we can see, shut our eyes, and think of nothing else."

They continued their trip to Rome and arrived in the early evening. He motored to her hotel. It was arranged that

Ben would pick her up later and they would dine in the small hideaway they discovered earlier.

The note from Gumper read: "Where the heck have you been? I heard about Como but thought you would hurry back. I am a lousy bodyguard if you can give me the slip so easily," and it was signed by Gumper.

When he rang Gumper, the latter was not in his room so Ben left a note in Gumper's box. It read, "Got back early this evening. Had a wonderful time. We are dining at the Dorando. You can join us later unless you have found your own girlfriend."

On the way out from his hotel, he ran into John Sergi who stopped Ben briefly to talk to him.

"It's pretty well wrapped up now, Washington figures. We've managed to get a crew over to where the yacht blew up and someone into Sarka to check. There was some debris, that's all."

"It was tough we lost Sebastian Giorgio," Ben said.

"Yes, I know," Sergi agreed. "The woman Talya Laylo is under the impression he was so close to death he had very little knowledge as to what had happened."

"It was unfortunate we could do so little," Ben added.

When they parted, the diplomatic John Sergi failed to ask anything about Regina Terchenka or when Ben was ready to return stateside. But they both knew the question of returning would be discussed shortly.

As long as he had his way, Ben knew he would not permit the closing out of the investigation and the chances were that Mark Crescent would maintain a continuous check on him for a lengthy period. They pretty well accounted for the elimination of Bartholomew Free, Manfred and others in the category of generally all others. However, there was no certainty that some member or members of the party had temporarily left the yacht to travel in Sarka or elsewhere. However, these speculations could continue forever. It would be similar to the continuous investigation of European Fascists or Nazis who disappeared, presumably dead. The most important item for consideration, Ben felt, was the relationship of Operation Baffle with established governments, and whether another Gregory Stavros would arise in the future from the ashes.

It was at Regina Terchenka's hotel that Ben saw his Washington acquaintance, Myles Bancroft.

Ben approached him, saying, "It is almost prophetic that we should meet again in a lobby, Mr. Bancroft."

"Ahem, yes, yes," he smiled pleasantly. "I understand Miss Terchenka was here, were you aware?"

There was an answer Ben had for this, that no one had been more aware than he of Regina Terchenka's presence, but he glossed over it with, "Yes, I've been seeing her. I am to have dinner with her this evening."

"A marvelous woman, a marvelous woman." Bancroft, it was noticeable, had a weakness for repetition. "And you, Mr. Ford, I have heard much about you. You are to be congratulated. It was a splendid performance." He placed his hands on his stomach in an elder statesman fashion. "I am sure that our friend, Mark Crescent, was pleased. How is he, by the way?"

"I spoke to him briefly, and he seemed fine."

When Ben mentioned his meeting with Myles Bancroft to Regina at dinner, she seemed mildly upset. "Yes, I know he is here; I saw him. I find him a pompous fool." And she seemed to want to end it there.

They would not shake the thought of Myles Bancroft, however, that easily; his presence, as in the past, seemed ubiquitous, once having been started. He appeared at a table in the same dining room, waving wildly in their direction. Ben felt him less pompous than he did unusual. Ben wondered how Bancroft would appear as some sort of impersonator. A fat one, at that. There was something that grabbed at Ben's senses as Bancroft sat a short distance from them.

Regina stated her displeasure when Ben continued to gaze in Bancroft's direction. "A rule of etiquette, Ben, is that it is not proper to stare at someone. It makes that person uncomfortable."

Laughing at this remark as it applied to Myles Bancroft, Ben said: "Our Mr. Bancroft seems the least upset. And as a rule of etiquette says he should not be reading the paper at the table and which he certainly is."

"Touché, you are right," Regina spoke, and did not pursue the subject further.

"If I take you for a ride now, Regina, will you thank me later?"

She blushed: "You are horrible, Ben."

"You misunderstand," he protested.

They both laughed in their happiness, and instead, decided to walk again in the park. They would melt into the joy of Rome. There was a dark greenness of the evening in the plants and grass. It was the artificial light that made these things seem greener than in the daytime. But there is a splendor in the night that cannot be seen or captured during the day; even the perfume of the flowers seem different. The world spun this day almost happily on its axis. Disturbing news had been slight. The lovers had no more of political discussions. They walked and laughed together.

Then Bancroft was in the pathway before them again. And a noticeable uneasiness came over Regina.

"Can he be everywhere?" she asked.

Ben, however, approached him with a remarkable

constraint for a Romeo startled in his amorous adventure.

"My dear Mr. Bancroft," he said, "it is a pleasure to meet again."

Bancroft smiled: "Ahem, yes." And he accepted Ben's hand that was extended to him.

And here and now began the revelation of Myles Bancroft. Whatever game he was playing had ceased. The hour struck in the bells of the churches of Rome. Bancroft stood immobile, for he was aware that Ben understood and knew. The lights of the park splashed down upon their faces. The three people seemed an eerie blue as the blue that Bancroft was wearing.

Ben withdrew his hand, slowly.

"Gregory Stavros," he said.

And the pretender Bancroft spoke firmly and decisively: "We finally meet face to face, Mr. Ben Ford."

Regina recoiled, for she saw the gun in Stavros' hand.

"You see, Regina, as I told you. Your Mr. Ford has proven too bright for us to continue to fool. He has felt the coldness of my hands. That is the finger with no life to it." Stavros removed the false small finger of his right hand, displaying his mutilated hand. "How did you know, Mr. Ford? Be so kind as to tell me."

"You dropped your glove that time in Barrymore."

The quietness about them remained. Stavros had chosen a secluded spot to meet them.

"Yes, it was careless of me." Stavros gazed from Ben's face to his gun. "Unfortunately, you have succeeded, but I cannot have the winner take all. You see, I love Regina Terchenka, too."

Ben Ford never felt the bullet noiselessly exploded from Stavros' gun. Regina had thrown herself between them and caught the full impact. And she slumped slowly to the ground, clasping her breast.

But before Stavros could fire again, there was another

explosion and this could be heard. It was from Gumper's .38. The bullet penetrated Stavros' head on the bridge of the nose between the eyes. He was dead before his body struck the ground.

"Regina, Regina," Ben cried, as he cradled her head in his knees. "Why did you do it?"

"It is better this way, Ben," she whispered. "It could never be. I loved you from the first day I saw you in San Francisco, Ben. You did not know it, did you?"

"Regina, please, you will be well. You will, won't you?"

"The air hostess on the ground beside you, Ben. Don't you remember?"

And he did remember. She had seemed so familiar, he recalled.

"I was their chosen agent on the ground, if Free had failed. I did not understand their wickedness. Always forgive me. I love you. Ben, I love you, you will remember."

Ben said sadly: "It is a terrible time, Regina, if I can hate that which I love dearly."

But she did not see or hear him.

Eighteen

FROM THE TIME of Ben's visit to her in Brindisi, Talya recovered until she was released and journeyed to Rome to see Ben.

Her kind, warm face did much to make Ben forget his unhappiness. Here was a woman who had witnessed so much pain and had been struck by the same loss of one loved dearly, and yet maintained a spirit and determination that might easily have been crushed in others.

It seemed strange at first that she had not known Regina and he learned the truth of the matter from Talya.

"Stavros maintained this separation as much as possible among those he had working for him–or forced to work for him. I knew there was another woman, Ben, but I never learned the name or who she was."

"It was not intended that Regina would come to Sarka?"

"Not that I know of. On their yacht, there were discussions between Stavros and Free. They spoke of a woman in Rome–very carefully. I think, Ben, she was supposed to hold you there."

"I've thought of that," he replied.

"When you came to Rome, they learned of it and it must have been at that time they directed Regina to follow you."

Ben was quiet for a while. He had suspected as much.

"It seemed strange at the time," he said, "the sudden, unexpected meeting. If only I had suspected at the time, things might have ended differently."

"Perhaps," she said sorrowfully, "if I had put two and two together, I might have realized, Ben, but I didn't."

"You should not think this way, Talya. You, who have suffered so much in the past, need no excuses."

"At least, Ben, you must realize she did not detain you, or expose your trip to Sarka."

"You're right, Talya. At that particular moment, if she had said anything, I could never have succeeded. And both Coranis and I would be dead."

"And I, as well," Talya said, pensively.

Ben noticed the change that had come over Talya since the ending of the episode. For a long period of time, she was forced to playact. Was this not the fact of agents, that their lives were a continuous performance in unreality? He could see her in a different light. If she had been so beautiful as he had known her, she was more devastatingly beautiful now. Her new charm was in her self-assurance and candidness. A tremendous burden was lifted from her shoulders, the constant demand that she be living a lie. Trapped by the love for her brother, she was forced to offer herself for his safety–which had been to no avail and was now past.

"What are your plans, Talya?" Ben asked.

"It may seem strange," she replied, "but I do have something I have been wanting to do for so long. I shall return to Honolulu and paint and teach. I miss the smell of the paints and the touch of the brush on the canvas. I shall return to the Islands. That is, after I have testified, and the government says

I may go."

"They shall," Ben assured her. "And you, perhaps, will get married and raise many children of your own."

"We shall see," she replied. "Do you think a man would want me now, Ben?"

Ben smiled as he held her long warm fingers in his hand.

"You are a most beautiful woman, Talya. Any man lucky enough to find you must count you as his finest blessing. You need not fear." With a firmness that came from his heart, he said: Talya, if ever you need any help, you must call on me."

Dr. Flair, relaxed and sedate, his legs crossed as he sat, the cuffless trousers hanging casually, spoke paternally with Ben Ford.

"I can understand your feelings, Ben, and I must say I sympathize with what you have experienced. However, we must go on. This seems the fact of life. We go on. Then the years pass and we're on a different plateau. What we see now looks different after the passage of a year or so. I cannot hope to remember every second of the sixty seconds times sixty minutes times twenty-four hours of every day, thank God. But the highlights, here and there, I recall, mostly the more pleasant ones."

"Yes, I understand," Ben said quietly.

A month had passed since the confrontation in the park. Dr. Flair had not disturbed Ben's stay in Rome. Now he came on a business matter to meet with John Sergi, and set aside a time for a meeting with Ben.

"This company of Myles Bancroft, the Primary Investigation of Living Psychological Items, the Pi-Lpi, it was weird, I know. Bancroft felt he had taken us in and, in the long run, perhaps he did. We were onto him, you know?"

Flair raised his eyebrows and when Ben did not reply, he continued.

"The unfortunate fact was, we did not realize what he was up to. The idea of using his company–a front to contact scientists in different parts of the country, worked well for him. He was lucky, no doubt. Many things could have happened to tip his wagon, but they didn't. That is the point, too. With all our vigilance, we must be always on guard for the crafty individuals who could perpetrate such a dastardly act and succeed, simply because they kept rolling sevens one after the other. The stakes are so large now."

Ben shifted uneasily. "You spoke of this Mr. Tao Sing."

"I am coming to that," Flair said, the tips of the fingers of his open hand touching the other similarly before him.

"Of course, this device, ingenious, perhaps, but nevertheless, simple, may have worked. And, if it had, the resultant detonation could have been to some degree destructive to the several miles radius they claimed. This may be the typical adversary exaggeration. The fact does stand out, however, that Operation Baffle was successful to a very definite degree. The fact that a highly devised plan could circumvent the preparedness and protection we have employed scares us–certainly scares me. I think we are in an age when we must be ever more watchful for plots against us, the conception of which are established over a period of years.

"Considering what has happened, we can readily realize the consternation if, say, an enemy were able to install twenty or thirty monstrous weapons secretly and strategically throughout the United States."

With a nervous laugh that seemed uncommon to him, he said: "We might be in store for bloody, dirty, blackmail. Especially where present-day electronics hardware could permit someone to have the control of a weapon from a remote area. You can see the horror of their success."

"What is the answer?" Ben asked. "Greater security?"

"Yes, vigilance. Complete disarmament, perhaps. Worldwide vigilance, perhaps." Somewhat deliberately, Flair continued. "You see why everyone is important to us. We need you, Ben, just as we need every good man's help."

Flair pursed his lips. "As for Sing, the Pi-Lpi connection was of great aid to us here. At the present time, we feel that with his death, the book has been closed."

Ben was curious. "How did it happen?"

Flair explained: "It was not simple. An agent of ours reported the meeting between Stavros and Tao Sing. It meant little to go by since he was unaware of Stavros' identity. The meeting occurred outside Tientsin. We scoured for every bit of information we could turn up. We made careful inquiries through all our offices. You can imagine how tremendously important this was to us. Where did Operation Baffle commence from; where did it end? This was our primary concern. We were uncertain if, in Bancroft's death, we had seen the end of the miscreants. Would they pop up elsewhere with another devilish scheme? Could we be sure that this escapade was not a cover-up for something worse? It was evident that, if a world power was not behind the scheme, someone, at least with the capacity within his grasp, gave great assistance and cooperation to Bancroft. Otherwise, how were the yachts, the money, the transportation available to them?

"Finally, after days of searching, a newspaper in Paris, *Le Soleil*, dug up a dispatch regarding the meeting of a Stavros with Tao Sing. The pieces in the jigsaw puzzle started to fall in place.

"Sing, you see, in his position as a Special Organizer, was able to provide the means for Stavros. No doubt, they had worked together on this matter for a seriously long time. Within a day or so, we were able to confirm Sing's relationship with Pi-Lpi. You might say, we were fully convinced then that he was our man, and the final source of the connivance."

"And his death?" Ben asked. "You spoke of his death."

"There was a particularly strange aspect to that," Flair replied. "We felt his apprehension was necessary. But how, and was it possible? After all, he was a member of a closed society with whom we were not on especially good terms." Flair rubbed his forehead contemplatively; he showed some doubts on this matter. "We are not sure here what exactly happened. Suffice it to say, there was some falling out between Sing and at least some members of their organization. Whether he had failed on a mission they had entrusted to him, or they had become wary of his scheming, or even possibly, when outside opinion fell upon them, they were shaken by a possible link of Sing to themselves–it is hard to say–he fled from Tientsin to Indonesia. You can imagine our astonishment when we learned of this. It seemed possible that he might be forced into the open where we might put our hands on him and question him." Flair sat upright and his eyes sought the light along the lead-beaded stained glass window. "We received a report, fully substantiated, that Tao Sing was shot one evening as he strolled from his car to a scheduled meeting. His body was quickly carried off and nothing further was heard about him."

That evening, Ben Ford learned of his new assignment and his recall to Washington. Dr. Flair spoke with Ben and John Sergi regarding the details and the final wrap-up of the facts on Operation Baffle.

Thus ended the basic machinations of Operation Baffle. The evenings had grown cooler in Rome. The days continued warm. Still, the azure of the sky remained, and the life of the city retained its placid contentment.

Things could have been different for Ben. But he accepted what was left to him and the last thing he wanted to do.

On his drive along the highway to Como, he found time to contemplate.

A little of his thoughts went to Gumper back in San Francisco. No doubt, he would see Gump again. His play with the .38 had saved Ben's life. Gump may refer to it as part of the day's work; it meant much more to Ben. On a foggy day in San Francisco Gump felt the pain in his shoulder, compliments of the despicable Bartholomew Free, but it did not prevent him from continuing on his patrol. He looked on his scar as a memento to the successful elimination of the Operation Baffle crowd.

Mark Crescent was a good guy; it would be great to see him again. And Ben could not forget Clarissa Neale. She was Ben's idea of the greatest secretary in the world. It would be a kick in the back if she were married now. He doubted it, but the day would come, he knew. One thing he would definitely do–this was indisputable–was take her out to dinner if she'd permit him. A glorious gal.

Kyle Sanders would have to fill Ben in on a few things. He had heard about Kyle's making it in record time to Los Angeles to intercept Walter Buswell.

Buswell and the rest of the unfortunate pawns for Myles Bancroft had been quietly made aware of their being duped. They hoped to return to their normal lives.

The same applied to Talya. Ben spoke to Dr. Flair and received his assurance in the matter. Some things had to be straightened out, but her assistance in aiding Ben at the risk of her life would go a long way.

If only he might see Coranis and Pesce again. This was impossible; the time now did not allow. But his prayers went out to them; the one on land, the other on the waters of the Adriatic.

Ben did not go the full distance to Como. He stopped at

the field where he had chased after Regina Terchenka. This was the end, he knew, of their relationship.

She had said to remember that day, that time, and he returned for that reason. But it was no good, he knew, even though he did it for her. It was killing him to walk through the long grass, and the flowered hillside from which they had earlier gazed down upon the quiet country. He came to the spot they had known so well. He could see all of the beautiful Italian country and the movements of a warm Italian day.

He remained until the sky darkened.

www.ingramcontent.com/pod-product-compliance
Lightning Source LLC
Chambersburg PA
CBHW071924130726
47909CB00014B/2577